Every muscle in Ford's body tensed with anticipation as Olivia slowly turned to face him.

It had been four months since he'd last seen his wife, four months that he'd spent hounding U.S. Marshals, trying to get a lead on Olivia's whereabouts. He'd finally found her, and he wanted to rush forward and pull her into his arms, but he knew she wouldn't thank him if he did. Just as he knew she wouldn't thank him for finding her. He'd broken one too many promises, ignored her one too many times. When she'd called to tell him she was entering witness protection, she'd said it was for the best. A clean break.

It hadn't been clean for Ford. It had been painful, filled with regrets and rife with a million lost opportunities.

"Ford. You shouldn't be here," she said quietly.

"But I am."

PROTECTING THE WITNESSES:

New identities, looming danger and forever love in the Witness Protection Program.

Twin Targets–Marta Perry, January 2010
Killer Headline–Debby Giusti, February 2010
Cowboy Protector–Margaret Daley, March 2010
Deadly Vows–Shirlee McCoy, April 2010
Fatal Secrets–Barbara Phinney, May 2010
Risky Reunion–Lenora Worth, June 2010

Books by Shirlee McCoy

Love Inspired Suspense

Die Before Nightfall
Even in the Darkness
When Silence Falls
Little Girl Lost
Valley of Shadows
Stranger in the Shadows
Missing Persons
Lakeview Protector
*The Guardian's Mission
*The Protector's Promise
Cold Case Murder
*The Defender's Duty
**Running for Cover
Deadly Vows

*The Sinclair Brothers
**Heroes for Hire

Steeple Hill Trade

Still Waters

SHIRLEE McCOY

has always loved making up stories. As a child, she daydreamed elaborate tales in which she was the heroine—gutsy, strong and invincible. Though she soon grew out of her superhero fantasies, her love for storytelling never diminished. She knew early that she wanted to write inspirational fiction, and began writing her first novel when she was a teenager. Still, it wasn't until her third son was born that she truly began pursuing her dream of being published. Three years later she sold her first book. Now a busy mother of five, Shirlee is a homeschool mom by day and an inspirational author by night. She and her husband and children live in Washington and share their house with a dog, two cats and a bird. You can visit her Web site at www.shirleemccoy.com, or e-mail her at shirlee@shirleemccoy.com.

Shirlee McCoy
DEADLY VOWS

Steeple
Hill®

Published by Steeple Hill Books™

Special thanks and acknowledgment to
Shirlee McCoy for her contribution to the
Protecting the Witnesses miniseries.

STEEPLE HILL BOOKS

Steeple
Hill®

Recycling programs
for this product may
not exist in your area.

ISBN-13: 978-0-373-67410-7

DEADLY VOWS

Copyright © 2010 by Harlequin Books S.A.

www.SteepleHill.com

Printed in U.S.A.

In you, O Lord, I have taken refuge; let me never be put to shame, deliver me in your righteousness. Turn your ear to me, come quickly to my rescue; be my rock of refuge, a strong fortress to save me.

—Psalms 31:1-2

To Marge Garrison.
Thank you for the warm hospitality and love
you show to all who enter Starr Road Baptist
Church. The love of Christ surely shines from you,
welcoming all to come and be part of His family.

PROLOGUE

MEMO: Top Secret, Top Priority
TO: FBI Organized Crime Division
FROM: Jackson McGraw, Special Agent,
       Chicago Field Office
DATE: March 20, 2010
RE: Operation Black Veil

At 4:00 P. M. EST, Ford Jensen, estranged husband of Olivia Jarrod, boarded a plane heading for Billings, Montana. Despite repeated requests to cease, Jensen continues to search for his wife. We have people in place to tail him when he arrives, but there is to be no contact between agents and Jensen unless absolutely necessary. For his safety and the safety of our witness, it is imperative Jensen not be seen as a potential trail to Olivia. Our mystery informant confirms that the Martino crime family has offered a reward to the person or persons who are able to find and assassinate Ms. Jarrod. To maintain the witness's safety, the U.S. Marshal Service has been contacted and the witness has been relocated from Billings.

Our informant believes that, in the event the Martino crime family does not succeed in its attempts to find and silence Ms. Jarrod, a hit will be arranged upon Ms. Jarrod's return to Chicago for Vincent "Bloodbath" Martino's trial. We are working closely with the U.S. Marshal Service to ensure Ms. Jensen's safety before, during and after the trial. There is to be no discussion or communication about the trial or witness outside of secure channels. Any questions or information regarding the Martino crime family are to come directly to me.

We continue to seek the identity of our mystery informant, but must not do anything that will jeopardize our position with her. No overt movements toward revealing her identity are to be made. We will continue to move within secure channels to gain more information. If you have any information, be advised that it must be shared only with Special Agent McGraw. The sole purpose of our task force is to protect our witness and to put Vincent

Martino behind bars where he belongs. To that end, every effort must be made to continue to receive information regarding the Martino family.

Questions or information regarding this matter are to be directed to Special Agent McGraw.

ONE

She'd popped.

Olivia Jarrod turned sideways and stared at her reflection, not sure if she should be elated or horrified. The flat plane of her stomach was gone. In its place was a subtle roundness that was emphasized by her fitted T-shirt. She placed her hands on the bump, imagining tiny hands and feet, translucent skin, a swiftly beating heart.

Her baby.

And Ford's.

She frowned, pulling the fabric taut against her abdomen as she turned from side to side. Thinking about Ford was something she tried not to do. The last few months had been difficult enough without reliving her failed marriage, thinking about the year she and Ford had been separated or dwelling on the last time she'd seen him.

She frowned again, turning away from the mirror and the telltale evidence of just how easily

she'd fallen for her husband's charming ways
again. She still didn't know why he'd shown up on
the doorstep of her Chicago bungalow just a few
days after Christmas. Had he been lonely in their
penthouse? Had he decided to fight for their
marriage?

Olivia had asked herself the same questions over
and over again in the days after she'd fled Chicago,
but she had no answers. All she knew for sure was
that Ford didn't want kids. Too much trouble, he'd
said years ago. Too many complications. He had
too much riding on his career and too little time to
devote to the mess and chaos children brought.

He'd be shocked if he found out he was going
to be a father.

Appalled.

Angry.

There were plenty of words Olivia could think
of that would describe Ford's reaction to impeding
fatherhood. None of them were good.

It was a good thing she knew it. Otherwise, she'd
pick up the phone and do what she knew she wasn't
supposed to. She'd call Ford. She'd tell him that in
a few short months he was going to be a father.

And she'd probably end up dying because she'd
contacted him.

After all, wasn't that the first rule of witness
protection?

No contact with anyone or anything from the past.

People who followed the rule lived. People who didn't died. It was as simple as that.

What wasn't simple was forgetting the past. Moving on. Letting go. She'd loved Ford for a long time. Even during their yearlong separation, she'd loved him, longed for his company and prayed that someday things would be different and they could be together again.

God hadn't answered that prayer.

But He *had* given Olivia something she'd always dreamed of. A baby. She needed to focus on that. Forget about everything else.

Which was exactly why she shouldn't be thinking about Ford.

As the key witness in the prosecution's murder case against Chicago crime family scion Vincent "Bloodbath" Martino, Olivia couldn't afford to make a mistake. Entering witness protection would only keep her safe as long as she followed the rules, and following the rules was only easy when she didn't dwell on the things she could no longer have. Like a relationship with the only man she'd ever loved, a man who'd broken her heart a hundred times but who still deserved to know he was going to be a father.

"Just stop it!" she muttered, grabbing her waitress

uniform off the bed and shoving it into the hamper. It had been a long day. A long couple of weeks, really. Being relocated from Billings, Montana, to Pine Bluff, Montana, had knocked her off kilter. Although, it was more the reason for the relocation rather than the move itself that had shaken her. Two women in witness protection had been murdered in Montana. Both women had green eyes and were around Olivia's age. The U.S. Marshals weren't sure if Olivia had been the true target of the attacks. The fact that she had blue eyes rather than green made the chances slim, but Micah McGraw, Olivia's contact in the marshal's office, hadn't wanted to take any chances.

So she'd been moved.

Quickly.

So quickly she hadn't had time to say goodbye to some of the friends she'd made in Billings or to tell her church family there that she was leaving. Nearly four months of pretending to be someone she wasn't, blending into a new community, and it was over. She'd packed a small bag, climbed into a waiting car and been whisked away.

And now she was tired. Jumping at shadows. Imagining danger around every corner.

She sighed, grabbing a sweater and throwing it over her T-shirt. What she needed was a cup of tea, a few hours of mindless television and a good night's sleep. She'd feel better in the morning.

The telephone rang as she walked into the living room, and she jumped, her heart racing.

"For goodness' sake, Olivia. It's just the phone," she mumbled as she lifted the receiver and pressed it to her ear. "Hello?"

"Olivia? It's Lorna Scott. I know this is short notice, but our preschool ballet teacher is sick. Any chance you can fill in for her?" Lorna asked, her tone brusque. Director of Pine Bluff's YMCA program, she was a frequent patron of the diner where Olivia worked, and often stopped in for breakfast during Olivia's shift. She'd been the first one in years to ask if Olivia was a dancer, and the question had sparked a long conversation about the YMCA's programs. It hadn't taken long for Lorna to offer Olivia a job as a substitute ballet teacher at the Y. It had taken Olivia a little longer to accept. She'd had to weigh the danger of participating in an activity connected to her previous life with the danger of making Lorna curious.

In the end, she'd decided that she'd rather accept the job than answer questions about why she couldn't. Too many lies made it too easy to make mistakes. "What time is the class?"

"Six."

Olivia glanced at her watch, hesitating. It was

only five. Plenty of time to get ready and go. She just wasn't sure she wanted to. She'd felt off all week. Nervous and even more on edge than usual. "I—"

"If you've got plans, I'm sure I can find someone else." There was a question in Lorna's words, and Olivia knew that refusing to take over the class meant explaining why she couldn't. Unfortunately, she had no real excuse.

"That's all right. I can come," she said, knowing she had to live her life as if she had nothing to be afraid of. As if she really was Olivia Jarrod from Hollywood, Florida, newly single and starting over with a new job in a new state.

"You're sure?"

"It's a forty-five-minute class, right?"

"That's right."

"Then no problem."

"See you at six."

Olivia hung up and paced to the front window. Outside, the sun was still high, its golden presence comforting. During daylight hours, Olivia felt almost safe. It was night that she dreaded. Darkness bred fear and stirred up memories she'd rather not dwell on. Not just of the murder she'd witnessed but of the years she'd spent alone waiting for Ford to come home from work, waiting for him to remember their anniversary or to wish her a happy birthday, waiting for her dreams of a happy home and loving family to come true. So much time wasted waiting for something that would never happen.

Too bad it had taken her so long to realize the truth. If she'd walked away two years into their marriage or three or even four rather than the ten it had taken, she and Ford would have been divorced a long time ago, and nothing that had happened in the past four months would have happened. She wouldn't have let Ford into her house, wouldn't have believed that he might really want something different from their marriage than what they'd had. She wouldn't have been so hurt when he'd interrupted a conversation about their future to take a business phone call.

And she wouldn't have run from her Chicago home and straight into a scene out of a crime drama—two men walking near the river, the moon bright and full above them. One pulling a gun, pointing it at the other's head and firing. A body falling into the river. A face that Olivia recognized from the newspaper.

She shuddered, pushing the memory away. It was better to focus on the present and the future. As much as she wished she hadn't seen a man murdered in cold blood, she couldn't regret that night. It had given her a precious gift. *God* had given her a precious gift. She needed to focus on that and forget everything else.

"We'll be okay, baby. I have to believe that," she said. God had gotten her through that terrifying night. He'd get her through the next month, and He'd get her through Vincent Martino's trial.

Her stomach rumbled, reminding her that she hadn't eaten since lunch. It would be a good idea to grab something before going to the YMCA, but Olivia was afraid to. Her stomach hadn't been quite right since she'd gotten pregnant, and the months hadn't eased the discomfort. Her new obstetrician had assured Olivia that she'd be feeling better soon, but soon hadn't come yet.

Anxious and antsy, she grabbed the pregnancy book she'd left on the coffee table, thumbed to the section on the second trimester and tried to read, but one word bled into another and she couldn't make sense of any of it. Disgusted, she dropped the book back onto the table, grabbed her purse and jacket and opened the front door.

Outside, the day had turned cool, a brisk breeze stirring the trees and grass. Across the street, Maria and Joshua Silverman were herding their three kids into their 1950s ranch style home. Both waved before disappearing inside. Olivia knew a lot about them. That they'd married straight out of high school and had their first child a year later. That they were honest, hard working and that they'd believed every word Olivia had said about being newly divorced and looking to start over again. What she didn't know was what they'd think if they found out the truth. That most of what she'd told them was a lie. That she was a woman with a price on her head, and that at any moment one of Vincent Martino's thugs might end her life.

She shivered, pulling the jacket closed and glancing up and down the quiet street. Her contact with the U.S. Marshals had been limited since she'd been relocated, but she'd been assured she was under twenty-four-hour protection. Maybe so, but she didn't feel protected. She felt vulnerable and more alone than she'd ever been before. No matter where she went in Pine Bluff, no matter what she was doing, she felt exposed. As if a predator were hiding just out of sight, waiting to pounce.

It wasn't a good feeling, and when she spoke to Micah McGraw again, she was going to ask him just how much protection his team was providing.

"Headin' out for the night?" Jeb Carlson, Olivia's next door neighbor, called out from the window of his house, and she smiled. Maybe the marshals weren't watching, but Jeb sure was.

"I'm teaching at the Y."

"Pretty girl like you should be out having fun on a Friday night not working."

"Having fun won't pay the bills."

"You got a point there. You get the delivery?"

"What delivery?" Olivia went cold at the question, her heart beating rapidly. She hadn't ordered anything, and as far as she'd noticed, no packages had been left for her.

"Van pulled into your driveway a couple hours ago. Guy got out and grabbed something from the back. Thought he was going to leave it on your porch."

"There was nothing here when I got home."

"He left pretty quick. I put on my shoes and walked outside and the van was already gone. Probably realized he was at the wrong house and left. Happens sometimes."

"Yeah." But agreeing didn't make it so. *Maybe* there'd been a mistake. Or maybe the Martinos had found her.

Found her? Of course they hadn't found her.

If they had, she'd be dead.

Jeb was right. The van and delivery were simply a mix-up. Nothing sinister or scary about them at all.

"You okay, doll?" Jeb asked, and Olivia forced herself to smile and nod. Nothing was going on. Nothing that couldn't be explained. She really *did* need to stop jumping at shadows and imagining Martinos around every corner.

"I'm fine. I'd better head out, though."

"Don't work too hard. A lady in your condition needs her rest."

"My condition?" Olivia paused with her hand on the door to her car. She hadn't told anyone in Pine Bluff about the pregnancy. Though she'd shared with a few people in Billings, discussing the baby inevitably led to questions about the baby's father. Questions Olivia couldn't answer with any amount of truthfulness.

"Now, don't be worrying that I'll tell every Tom, Dick and Harry about it, but I've been around enough pregnant women to know one when I see one."

"I—" Olivia glanced down at the slight swelling of her stomach. Was it really that noticeable?

"Besides. I saw the pregnancy book on your table when you had me in for coffee the other day. I suppose it's that no-good ex-husband's child."

"Yes." She barely kept herself from correcting Jeb, from telling him that she wasn't divorced and that Ford wasn't no-good. That he was just too caught up in making money to care much about creating a family.

Or about her.

"Well, it's your business when you tell other people, but if you need anything, I'm right next door."

"Thanks, Jeb." Olivia got in the car and started the engine, her hand shaking. In Pine Bluff, keeping to herself was nearly impossible. The town was small, the people friendly and curious about the newcomer in their midst. Being standoffish or closed-mouthed would only make them talk about her more and that was the last thing Olivia wanted.

Blend in.

She could hear the words that had been pounded into her from the moment she'd agreed to enter the witness protection program. *Don't do anything that is going to get you noticed.*

That was a lot easier said than done when you were single and pregnant in small-town America. Soon, the little bulge of her stomach was going to grow. The baby that she'd been able to hide up to this point wouldn't be hidden any longer. When that happened, people *would* talk.

But, please, God, don't let any of Martino's men be around to hear it.

The sun dipped below distant mountains as Olivia drove across town, shrouding streets and alleys in shadows. As always, the darkness brought memories. The gun. The explosion of sound as it was fired point-blank into another man's head. Vincent Martino's cold face illuminated by moonlight. No matter how hard Olivia fought to let go of her old life, she couldn't rid herself of it. Perhaps that was why she felt so on edge, so nervous.

Streetlights did little to dispel the darkness or to chase away the memories, and Olivia was tense with anxiety as she pulled into the parking lot at the Y.

Housed in an old warehouse, the building was long and narrow, the parking lot large. A few cars were parked near the building, and Olivia pulled in close, hesitating a moment before opening her door. Maybe she should quit teaching at the Y, quit waitressing and lock herself in her house until the marshals came to take her to Vincent Martino's trial.

Go about your daily life as if nothing has changed. Keep up the appearance of normalcy. Don't give anyone a reason to think you have something to hide.

"Easy for you to say, Micah. You're not the one with the price on your head," she murmured as she forced herself to open the door and step out of the car. Evenings in Pine Bluff, Montana, had a richness to them. The sky seemed ripe with starlight, the distant mountains fading into deep azure sky. God's creation, filled with wonder and beauty, but Olivia could find no comfort in it.

She hurried toward the building, her pulse jumping as something scraped on the pavement behind her.

She didn't want to turn to look.

Then again, she didn't want to die with her back to her killer.

She whirled, ready to face down the threat, but the parking lot was empty of life.

Olivia took a step back, her eyes probing the shadows. Was someone there, waiting and watching? A U.S. Marshal, maybe? Or someone worse?

Skin crawling, the hair on the back of her neck standing on end, Olivia took another step back and then turned and ran toward the building. She yanked the door open with enough force to send it crashing against the wall and bounded into the foyer, her breath heaving, her heart racing.

"No need for quite that much of a hurry. You've got ten minutes before the class starts," Lorna Scott said, peering out of the office. Sixty, with short, dark hair cut into a pixie style, Lorna eyed Olivia with curiosity. "Is everything okay?"

"Fine. Everything is fine. The door just got away from me."

Lorna raised a dark eyebrow, but didn't comment. What could she say, short of calling Olivia a liar? "I'm glad you got here a little early. I need to talk to you about something. Come on in the office."

"What's up?"

"Someone was here looking for you. He said he was your husband," she said quietly, but the words seemed to fill the room, stealing Olivia's breath.

She swayed, grabbing a chair to steady herself. "That's impossible."

"I'm afraid it's not. He arrived just a half hour after I called you. Said his name was Ford, showed me a picture of you and asked if you worked here. I would have called to let you know, but I figured you were already on your way here."

"What did you tell him?"

"That you didn't work here. Can't say the lie sat very well, but I wasn't sure what kind of relationship you two had. I figured if he was the ex you told me about, you might not want him to know where you worked."

"I appreciate it, Lorna."

"Your private life is your private life. Besides, the guy looked a little dangerous. I was anxious to get him out of the building."

"Dangerous? Ford?" Olivia never would have described him as that. Successful, confident, too handsome for his own good, those were more apt descriptions.

"Maybe it was just the scar. You know how that is. Guy's got a scar on his face, he looks dangerous whether he is or not."

"Ford doesn't have a scar."

"Well, this guy did. On his right cheek. Didn't distract from his good looks, but it sure did make me wonder how he got it."

"It couldn't have been Ford, then." Which meant someone else had come to the Y looking for Olivia. Someone with a photograph of her.

"Maybe not, but someone was here, and it *was* you he was looking for. Want me to call the police?"

"No. That's okay. Listen, I hate to do this, but I'm not up to teaching tonight after all."

Lorna nodded, not bothering to ask why, not commenting again on the scarred man. She must have known things weren't right with Olivia. Maybe she'd even begun to suspect that the things Olivia had shared were only partial truths. "That's all right. I'll find someone else."

"Thanks." Olivia hurried from the office, her mind racing. She needed to get in the car and drive as fast and as far from Pine Bluff as she could. Once she put some distance between herself and the town, she'd call Micah and let him know that she'd been found.

She unlocked the car, started to pull the door open.

"Olivia?" The voice shivered through the darkness, gritty and deep and as familiar as her own.

Ford. Her husband. The father of her child. The

man she'd tried so hard to forget during her four months in witness protection. Behind her. Waiting for her to turn and face him.

Not the kind of danger she'd expected, but danger nonetheless.

"If you get in the car and drive away, I'll just follow you." There was little emotion in the words, just a cold statement of fact.

She could turn around and face him now or she could run and face him later. Either way, she'd have to deal with him. Ford never gave up on something he wanted, never stopped pushing for a win. This time, though, the drive to succeed might cost him more than he bargained for. If Olivia didn't convince him to go back to Chicago, it might cost them both their lives.

TWO

Every muscle in Ford Jensen's body tensed with anticipation as Olivia slowly turned to face him. It had been four months since he'd last seen his wife, four months that he'd spent hounding FBI agents and U.S. Marshals, trying to get a lead on Olivia's whereabouts. He'd finally found her, and he wanted to rush forward and pull her into his arms, but he knew she wouldn't thank him if he did. Just as he knew she wouldn't thank him for finding her. He'd broken one too many promises, ignored her one too many times. When she'd called to tell him she'd seen a murder and that she was entering witness protection, she'd said it was for the best. A clean break.

It hadn't been clean for Ford. It had been painful, filled with regrets and rife with a million lost opportunities.

"Ford. You shouldn't be here," she said quietly, her hand resting on the door of a dark blue Ford.

"But I am."

"I've got some dangerous people after me. You don't want to get caught up in my troubles."

"I already am. I have been from the night you called to tell me you planned to disappear from my life." He walked toward her, letting the streetlight fall on his face.

She frowned, her gaze dropping to his cheek and the ridge of scar tissue that bisected it. "The Martino family did that to you?"

"That's not important."

"Of course it is. We may not be together anymore, but I still care about you, and I'd hate to think that you were hurt because of me."

"Maybe the fact that you feel that way means we *should* still be together."

"I care, Ford. I've never pretended otherwise, but we both know it's not enough. Pouring love into you is like pouring it into a black hole. It's never filled and it never returns what it takes."

"No need to hold your punches, Liv. Why not tell me exactly how you feel?" But she was right, that was exactly how it had been. Olivia giving affection and love. Ford taking it. He hadn't meant it to be that way, hadn't even realized it was that way until she'd walked out of their Chicago penthouse nearly fourteen months ago.

"If being blunt will get you back in your car and back in Chicago, that's what I'll be."

"It won't." He moved toward her, searching her face, wondering about the dark circles beneath her eyes, the hollows in her cheeks. Was she eating right? Sleeping well?

"Please, Ford, don't make this difficult. You being here has put both of us in danger. I've made a clean break from my old life, started a new one. I can't have that jeopardized by your presence."

"And you think I'm just going to walk away and leave you to face Vincent Martino's trial alone?" he asked, knowing that was probably what she *did* think. He'd walked away plenty during their marriage, left her alone more times than he cared to admit. Maybe God hadn't completely given up on Ford, because the second chance he'd been praying for was happening. A second chance to love Olivia the way she deserved to be loved, to create the home she'd often talked about. The one he'd stopped believing in the day his alcoholic father had walked out and left him and his three siblings to care for their drug-addicted mother. A home filled with love and laughter.

"You don't have a choice. Neither do I. The U.S. Marshals have made it clear that I'm to have no contact with anyone from my previous life. Not you. Not my parents. Not my friends. Not the people I worked with. No one."

"There's something you and the marshals seem

to have forgotten. I'm not part of your previous life. You and I are still married."

"We've been separated for over a year."

"We've been separated for less than four months. Or have you conveniently forgotten what happened in December." The words were out before Ford could stop them, and he regretted them immediately.

Olivia stiffened, her eyes flashing with anger and hurt before she turned away.

"Liv—"

But she was already opening the door and sliding into her car.

He grabbed the door before she could close it. "Olivia, I'm sorry. That didn't come out right."

"What way would have been right?" she asked, then sighed and shook her head. "Never mind. I've got to go call my contact in the marshals. He'll want to know you've found me. If he doesn't already."

"If he doesn't, I'm going to want to know why not."

"There's no need to get macho and protective, Ford. The marshals have done a great job of keeping me safe so far. I'm sure they're not shirking their duty now."

"Two women in witness protection have been murdered in the past few months. Someone somewhere is shirking his duty." The fact that both women had the hair like Olivia's had made Ford all the more desperate to find her. There was no doubt Vincent Martino's family planned to silence Olivia. They'd nearly killed Ford trying to find out where she was. Whether or not they'd mistaken the other two women for Olivia was something the FBI and the U.S. Marshals refused to speculate on. At least in their conversations with Ford.

"Micah told me two women had been killed, but I'm not sure their deaths mean the Marshals aren't doing their jobs."

"Micah McGraw?" Ford had spoken to him several times, but the way Olivia said the guy's name made him sound like an old friend rather than someone being paid to keep her safe. The surge of jealousy he felt at the thought was as unwelcome as the guilt that had been eating at him since Olivia had run from her Chicago home and disappeared into the night while he discussed a real estate venture with an associate. He'd hung up the phone and tried to follow, but she'd been long gone before he'd managed to get out the front door. If he'd ignored his cell phone when it rang, if he'd refused to take the call, Olivia wouldn't have been out walking beside the river when Vincent Martino committed cold-blooded murder.

"Yes. Micah is my contact, and he's not going

to be happy to know I hung around chatting with you when I should have been home packing. Thanks for caring enough to search for me, Ford, but as you can see, I'm fine." She offered a quick smile, started to shut the door, but he held it open, leaning in so he could look in her eyes.

"I'm not walking out of your life, Olivia."

"Why not? You were happy enough to let me walk out of yours fourteen months ago. Besides, our marriage has been over for a long time. What happened after Christmas was a mistake. It's best if we both forget it." She pulled the door from his hand, the sharp retort as she slammed it echoing through the parking lot.

Maybe Olivia was right. Maybe it was best if they both forgot what had happened in December. If they moved on with their lives, moved forward with the divorce that had seemed so inevitable when she'd packed a bag and walked out of their penthouse.

Maybe, but Ford didn't think so.

It took him several seconds to cross the parking lot and get into his car. By the time he started the engine, Olivia was pulling out onto the street, her blue Ford disappearing from view. He followed, thankful that they were driving through the small town of Pine Bluff rather than Chicago. No way would he have been able to keep her in sight otherwise. As much as he'd always loved city life, he had to admit there were benefits to the small towns and rural communities he'd visited during his search for Olivia. Slower pace of life, quieter atmospheres, people who noticed what was going on in their communities and who cared. If not for them, Ford wouldn't have known he was on the right track when he began searching for Olivia in Montana. The fact that two women who resembled Olivia had been murdered in the state had been reason enough to go there, but it wasn't until he'd shown Olivia's photograph to a few people in Billings who'd recognized her that Ford knew he should keep searching there.

Olivia pulled into the driveway of a 1920s bungalow, and Ford parked behind her, getting out of his car as she hurried to her front door. There was no doubt that she'd rather he leave, but Ford couldn't. There was too much history between them, too much love buried beneath layers of resentment and pain. He wasn't willing to give that up any more than he was willing to let Olivia face the danger she was in alone.

"Go home, Ford." Olivia shoved the key in the lock as he stepped onto the porch, her long dark hair falling across her face and hiding her expression.

"I can't." It was the truth.

He'd nearly been killed the day after Olivia went into witness protection. Martino's men had been brutal in their questioning. When he'd woken in the hospital, his only thought had been finding Olivia and making sure she was safe. It had taken him months to do it, but he'd finally succeeded, and there was no way he was going to walk away.

"Sure you can. Turn around, get back in the car and drive to Chicago."

"And forget that you're in danger? Forget that Chicago's most well-known crime family wants you dead?"

"You don't have to forget anything. You just have to remember that we're nothing to each other." She glanced over her shoulder as she stepped into the house, her expression hard, her gaze steely.

What had happened to the twenty-year-old with dreams in her eyes? The one who'd laughed when he'd nearly knocked her over while hurrying to an accounting class? She'd been dressed for ballet, her hair in a tight bun, a knit dress hugging her slender frame. Ford had picked up the books that had spilled from her arms, looked into her eyes and decided that being late for accounting class wouldn't be such a bad thing.

"Nothing? You used to tell me I was everything to you."

"You were. That was the problem. You were everything to me, and I was—"

Secondary.

She didn't say the word, but Ford knew she was thinking it. Hadn't he said it to her the day she'd asked for a divorce and walked out of his life?

My career is priority. Everything else is secondary.

The words seemed to hang in the air as Ford followed Olivia into the house. The walls were sage-green, the floor dark wood that was faded and nicked with time. There was little furniture in the living room. Just a love seat that faced the fireplace and a coffee table that held a few magazines and a book. Olivia grabbed the book as she walked past, shoving it into the table's only drawer.

A romance novel?

Probably.

He'd laughed when they'd been dating and he'd seen her reading one, but she'd just smiled and said romance was the perfect escape from the mundane world. He'd told her that a world with her in it could never be mundane.

When had he forgotten that?

"Olivia—"

She looked over her shoulder and met his gaze, her eyes empty of emotion. "I need to call Micah."

"I have a better idea." He grabbed her hand

before she could lift the phone. "How about we get in my car, drive to the nearest airport and fly to Paris? I've got a friend there who is willing to put us up until the trial."

"If we live that long."

"All we have to do is make it to the airport and onto a plane. There's no way the FBI will let any of the Martinos out of the country."

"They won't need to. The Martinos have enough money to hire an army to come after me. And they won't need an army. All it will take is one person to get the job done. If you were thinking clearly, you'd realize that."

She was right. He wasn't thinking clearly. Hadn't been thinking clearly since she'd called to tell him she was being put in protective custody and they'd never see each other again. "So, check in with Micah. Tell him I want to fly you out of the country. It seems to me the farther you are from the Martinos, the better."

The phone rang before Olivia could respond, and she answered, turning away from Ford as she spoke.

"Hello? Yes. He is," she said, glancing over her shoulder and frowning in Ford's direction. He didn't even bother pretending that he wasn't listening.

"I know. All right. I'll be ready." She hung up,

and turned to face Ford again. "I'm going to be re-located." *Thanks to you.*

She didn't say the last, but Ford could see the accusation in her eyes.

"I'd say I was sorry I found you, but that would be a lie."

"Since when did lying bother you?" she retorted, the words more resigned than venomous.

"I've never lied to you, Livy. Not before and not now."

"Maybe not." She offered a tired smile. "Look, I've got to pack and you've got to leave." She walked to the front door, her movements graceful and fluid. Even if he hadn't known she'd studied dance for twelve years, he would have thought she was a dancer. She carried herself with understated confidence that he'd always found alluring.

"I'll leave when you do."

"You don't have to stick around, Ford. The marshals will be here any minute."

"Maybe I should rephrase that. I'll leave *with* you. I didn't spend all this time searching for you to let you disappear again. Wherever you go, I'm coming."

"You can't."

"Of course I can," he responded. He'd been offered a place in the witness protection program after Martino's men had nearly killed him. When he'd learned he wouldn't be placed with Olivia, he'd refused. Finding her had been his first priority. His only one. Now his priority was making sure he didn't lose her again. No one, not the Martinos, not the FBI and not the U.S. Marshals would keep him from doing that.

"So let's say you can. That doesn't mean I want you to."

"You'd rather I let you face this alone?"

"I'd rather you'd stayed in Chicago. I'm sure your business is suffering without you there."

"I don't care about my business. I care about you."

She laughed, the sound short and sharp. "We both know that isn't true."

"Olivia…"

A quick rap at the door interrupted his words, and Ford was almost glad. There were so many things he wanted to say, so many ways he'd imagined saying them. Somehow, though, none of them seemed like enough. Not to convey what he felt or to express his sorrow for the pain he'd caused Olivia.

She started toward the door, but Ford put a hand on her arm. "I'll get it."

He was a foot away when the door swung open and two men stepped inside. Tall and dark-haired, the older of the two flashed his badge. "I'm U.S. Marshal Sebastian James."

"Ford Jensen."

"And I'm Olivia Jarrod," Olivia said, offering her hand to the tall, dark-haired marshal as if having marshals barge into her home was an everyday occurrence. For all Ford knew, it was.

"Nice to meet you, Ms. Jarrod. Marshal McGraw said he'd contacted you about relocation?"

"That's right."

"Good. You've got ten minutes to pack a bag. Then we'll head out. Mr. Jensen, you'll be going with Marshal Louis. He's going to escort you to Billings where you'll be briefed to enter the witness protection program."

"Sorry, but I'm staying with my wife."

"Wife? You two are separated, right?" The second of the two men spoke up, his gaze shooting from Ford to Olivia and back again.

"We are," Olivia said.

"We *were*."

"Sorry to have to break off the discussion, but we've got to get moving. Headquarters wants you both out of Pine Bluff. The sooner the better." Marshal James smiled but there was a hardness to his expression that Ford didn't miss. He seemed on edge, his gaze darting from one corner of the room to another as if he expected to find danger hiding there.

"You think the Martinos know Olivia is here?" Ford asked, his muscles tensing at the thought. The men they'd sent to question him about Olivia had been more than willing to murder to get what they wanted. That knowledge had driven Ford from Chicago to Atlanta, from there to Maryland and finally to Montana following leads from the private investigative firm he'd hired to help him with the search.

"If you found her, someone else might. Better to relocate now than regret that we didn't tomorrow."

"I just need to pack a few things, and I'll be ready to go," Olivia said, cutting into the conversation and stepping toward the hall.

"I'll give you a hand." Ford followed, ignoring the hard look she shot in his direction.

"Thanks, but I've been packing for myself for a long time."

"An extra set of hands will get it done more quickly, and I agree with the marshals. The sooner we all get out of here the happier I'll be."

"I'll work more quickly without a distraction."

"Is that all I am?" he asked quietly so that only Olivia could hear.

"We're in a hurry, Ford. I don't have time for word games or deep discussions about what you are to me."

She was right. They didn't have time to hash things out, but they would. There were things he needed to say, promises he still needed to keep. He'd been given a second chance. He wouldn't waste it. "Go ahead and pack. I'll wait here."

She nodded and disappeared into a room at the head of the hall. He wanted to stand in the threshold, watch her pack and assure himself that she wasn't going to disappear the way she had in December, but there'd been too many times in their marriage when he'd disregarded her feelings and ignored her requests. He wouldn't do it now.

"Mr. Jensen, I'm going to put in a call to our Billings office. We may be able to get the okay to move you and Ms. Jarrod together. I can't promise anything, though." Marshal James pulled a cell phone from his pocket.

"It doesn't matter what the Billings office says, I'm going with Olivia."

"Look, I understand how you feel, but—"

Glass shattered and something exploded, the living room filling with smoke and flames. Thrown backward by the force of the explosion, Ford slammed into the wall, the breath forced from his lungs. If he was hurt, he didn't feel it. All he felt was the panicked need to get to Olivia, to make sure she was alright. He scrambled to his feet, weaving a little as he moved into the hall.

"Olivia!" He shouted, the words lost in the crackle and hiss of the fire that was spreading toward him.

Olivia raced from the room, her face a pale oval in the thickening gloom. "What happened? Where are the marshals?"

"I don't know, but we've got to get out of here. Is there a back door?"

"Through the kitchen."

"Come on then," he grabbed her hand, tugging her past hot flames and into the kitchen. He'd never been a praying man, had never believed in anything but his own strength and determination, but over the past few months he'd started doing what he'd never thought he would, asking for a miracle. He'd gotten it. He'd found Olivia. Safe. Alive. Was it too much to ask for more?

Please, just let me get her out of here.

He pulled her through the kitchen, opened the back door, inhaling cool, fresh air.

"Ford, no," Olivia shouted. "They might be out there. Let's wait for the marshals. They'll know what to do."

The marshals.

Ford hadn't seen either since the explosion.

Were they alive?

He couldn't leave the house without being sure. Couldn't abandon two men to the flames.

"Wait here. I'll go see if I can find them," he said, stepping away from the door and the sweet promise of escape.

"You can't go back in there. The smoke is too thick. You'll never be able to find your way through it."

"I can't leave two men to die. Give me two minutes. If I'm not back by then, you're going to have to make a run for it."

"No!"

"I love you, Livy. I always have." He pressed a kiss to her lips and sprinted out of the kitchen and into the thickening smoke, the words echoing in his ears, reminding him of all the things he should have said, all the time he should have spent. He'd worked hard, made millions of dollars in hundreds of real estate deals, but he'd lost the only thing he'd ever truly valued.

Lost, but found again.

He couldn't die. Wouldn't die. Not when Olivia might still need him.

He dropped to his knees, smoke stinging his eyes and lungs and crawled back into the living room, praying that he would make it back to Olivia before the flames consumed the house and everything in it.

THREE

Two minutes.

One-hundred twenty seconds.

Such a short amount of time, but Olivia knew better than most that a few moments could change a life completely. In December, she'd celebrated Christmas alone, congratulating herself on not giving in to her parents' demands to fly to Florida to be with them. She'd dressed up on Christmas Eve and attended candlelight service, refusing to feel self-conscious about being there alone. Then she'd returned home and decorated a tiny Christmas tree, drank hot chocolate and danced to "The Nutcracker Suite." Alone and independent and almost happy to be that way.

And then it had all changed.

Ford had come knocking, telling her all the things he knew she wanted to hear. Somehow she'd fallen into the fantasy of renewal, glimpsed the dreams she'd given up on and let herself believe that he'd changed. Regret had come immediately, and she'd run outside and into more trouble than she'd ever imagined she could find. Now she was a puppet, pulled by invisible strings, going in directions she didn't want to.

She coughed, thick smoke filling her throat and burning her eyes. How long before the fire spread to the kitchen? How long before the entire house was engulfed in flames? Could she afford to wait any longer for Ford to return?

Could she live with herself if she left without him?

Lord, please, let him come back soon.

The prayer whispered through her mind as she grabbed a dish towel, soaked it and covered her mouth and nose. It wasn't just herself she needed to worry about. She had the baby to think of. An innocent life she needed to protect. But she couldn't just leave Ford and the two marshals to die.

She dropped to her hands and knees, crawling to the kitchen threshold. "Ford!" she shouted, but the words barely carried through the dish towel and over the crackling roar of the fire.

"Ford!" She tried again, and this time a shadow appeared in front of her. Broad and tall and darker than the thick smoke. Olivia blinked, scrambling backward.

"I thought I told you to leave!" Ford shouted, towering over her, one of the marshals held in a fireman carry over his shoulder. Another man followed close behind.

"I was worried," she said, standing, relief and fear mixing, stealing her breath and her strength. She put a hand on the wall, steadying herself.

"You could have worried from outside. Come on. The whole living room is in flames. It won't take long for it to spread to the roof."

"Let me go first." Marshal James limped out from behind Ford.

She followed him to the kitchen door, the smoke thicker, the room nearly black with it. She coughed, gagging on the moist, hot air she inhaled.

"Wait until I call for you," Marshal James said as he stepped outside. Several seconds passed as the fire in the living room crackled and hissed and the thick blackness intensified.

Ford pressed in close to Olivia, leaning out the door, still carrying the fallen man. "If he doesn't call us outside soon, we're walking out without the go-ahead. The way that fire is blazing, the whole place could collapse."

The imagine of the house shuddering, then falling in on itself flashed through Olivia's head. Not a pretty picture. Especially if she, Ford and Marshal Louis were still in the house when it happened.

"All right. We're clear. Come on," Marshal James said as he reappeared in the doorway and took Olivia's arm, gently guiding her down the back steps. "Are you okay, Ms. Jarrod."

"Fine. It's your partner I'm worried about," she responded, pulling off the wet cloth and turning to watch as Ford approached. Cool air bathed her cheeks, filled her lungs. She was safe. They were all safe. For now.

Ford stopped beside her, carefully lowering the unconscious marshal to the ground, and bending over him. "He's still breathing, but his head is bleeding a lot. We need to call an ambulance."

"Already done," Marshal James said, his voice raspy with smoke.

"Maybe we should wait at a neighbor's house until they come. I don't like the idea of Olivia being out here in the open." Ford put a hand on Olivia's shoulder, and she knew she should step away. He was her husband and the father of her child, but whatever else he'd been had died a long time ago. Allowing herself to believe differently would only make it harder to say goodbye.

"Go, but not to the neighbors. Find a ride out of town and keep going until you've put as much distance between yourself and this town as you can," Marshal James said, as he leaned over his partner. He didn't look at Olivia and Ford as he said it, and for a moment Olivia thought the smoke and heat had wreaked havoc on her brain cells.

"What are you saying, James? You want us to leave the program? Go out on our own?" Ford asked, frowning a little as he met Olivia's gaze.

"What I'm saying is that we've done a *great* job of keeping Ms. Jarrod safe." He looked up, his expression hard and grim. "Look, I could lose my job for saying this, but I'd rather lose my job than see you or your wife lose your life. There's a leak somewhere in the organization. We've suspected it for a while, but can't find it. If you stay in the program, there's no guarantee either of you will live to see the Martino trial."

"But—" Olivia began, the sound of sirens cutting off whatever question she planned to ask. Good thing, because she wasn't sure what to ask. What to say.

"Sounds like help is here. Better make your decision about what you want to do before they come back here."

"It's made. Thanks for the warning. Come on, Olivia. Let's go," Ford said, taking her hand and pulling her across the backyard.

"Go where?" Olivia asked, but she didn't resist his gentle grip. Didn't even try to pull away as they walked through the yard of the house behind hers.

"Like Marshal James suggested—far away from here."

A shout came from somewhere behind them, and Olivia's pulse jumped. She glanced back, saw the house nearly consumed by flames, dark figures spilling around the side and into the backyard. Firefighters? Police? More federal marshals?

"If we're going it alone, we'd better pick up the pace. You game?" Ford asked, and she looked up into his face. It wasn't often he asked an opinion and rare that he included anyone else in his plans. What was he thinking? Worrying about?

There was no time to ask.

No time for anything but a quick nod. "Yes."

They ran through the yard behind Olivia's, cut around the side of the house and out onto a sidewalk where a crowd of people stood staring at the flames that shot up into the black sky. If anyone watched Olivia and Ford race away from the scene, Olivia didn't notice. She was too busy trying to keep pace with Ford.

Dusk threw long shadows across the road as Ford pulled Olivia away from the crowd and further along the quiet street. At six foot two he was nine inches taller than Olivia, his long legs eating up the ground at a pace she normally wouldn't be able to match. Funny how motivating fear could be. Not only was Olivia able to keep up, but she thought she might just be able to beat Ford in a race.

Her legs ached, her lungs burned, but fear spurred her on.

A leak in the organization. Rather lose my job than see you dead.

The marshal's words chanted through Olivia's mind in time to the frantic beat of her heart. A leak in the U.S. Marshals? Was that how the two murder victims had been found?

Did it matter?

She'd been found. Any illusion she'd had that the marshals could keep her safe was gone. She wasn't safe. Wouldn't be safe as long as the Martino family thought they could keep her from the trial.

A sharp pain ripped through her side, and she gasped, bending over so suddenly Ford nearly pulled her off her feet before he was able to stop. Hunched over, gasping for breath, she grabbed her side. *Please, just let it be a cramp. Please don't let anything be wrong with the baby.*

"You okay?" Ford brushed hair from Olivia's face, his fingers lingering on her cheek. Warm. So familiar. More welcome than they should be. Would he be touching her with such kindness if he knew she was pregnant? Or would he turn and walk away, leaving her alone as he had so many times during their marriage?

"Fine," she managed to say as she straightened and moved away from his touch. Things were complicated enough. No way would she complicate them more by thinking about the past. Ford was her husband for now, the father of her baby forever, but he would never again be the man who'd held her heart in his hands.

"Are you sure?" He scanned her face, his eyes glimmering darkly in the dim streetlight.

"Yes. We'd better keep moving. The marshals will be looking for us." So would Martino's men, but giving voice to that fear would only make it more terrifying, and Olivia kept it to herself.

Ford glanced back the way they'd come, and frowned. "You're right. It doesn't look like anyone followed us, but that doesn't mean we're safe."

"We need to get out of town."

"I was thinking the same thing. The problem is, both our cars are back at your place."

"There's a train station the next town over. I'm sure someone would give us a ride there." She hadn't had much of a chance to build friendships in Pine Bluff, but she was sure that her neighbor Jeb would give her a ride if she asked. If not, one of her coworkers at the diner or someone from church might be willing to help.

"I've got two problems with that. The first is that we'd be putting someone else in danger. The second is that the train station is going to be the first place anyone searching for you will look. I saw a used car lot just outside of town. If I can get to it, I can buy us a ride."

"It's three miles from here. That's too far to walk with the marshals searching for us."

"The marshals aren't the only ones searching, and they're not the most dangerous. That's exactly why I'm going alone."

"You can't."

"Of course I can. Anyone searching for us will be looking for two people. They won't pay much attention to a lone guy wandering around town," he sounded confident and sure of himself, but that was how Ford always sounded. If he ever had doubts, he didn't let anyone know about them. If he had worries he didn't share.

"I don't think it's a good idea."

"It's the only one we have. There's a church up ahead. We'll see if it's open. If it is, you can stay there until I get back."

"Ford—"

"I don't like this any more than you do, Livy. I've spent months searching for you. I don't want to let you out of my sight, but I can't see any other way to get us out of Pine Bluff." He led her up the church's wide steps and pushed open the door, urging her inside.

"Maybe we should forget all about leaving town and go back to my house. The trial is only three weeks away. I'm sure the marshals can keep me safe until then," she said as she stepped into the brightly lit building. The wide corridor lined with doors was silent and empty but for several wooden benches lined up against the walls.

"They didn't tonight. And if there's really a leak like Marshal James said, they won't be able to. The best thing we can do is go underground and stay there until the date of the trial."

"For all we know, Marshal James is wrong and there is no leak. It's possible the Martinos followed you or that they found me the same way you did."

"I've been trekking back and forth across Montana since a lady in Billings recognized your photograph. I'm talking miles of open road with nothing but blue sky and mountains as far as the eye could see. If someone had been following me I would have known it."

"So it's just a coincidence that you found me and then Martino's men did?" Olivia sank onto one of the benches, suddenly too tired to stand, too tired to argue and almost too tired to care whether she and Ford made it out of town.

"I don't know. I just know I wasn't followed." Ford sounded as tired as Olivia felt. That was so unlike him, so different from the constantly moving, constantly energized man she'd married that Olivia studied his face, looking for some sign of what he'd been through in the months since she'd gone into witness protection. Aside from the scar that bisected his right cheek, he looked the same. Handsome. Strong. Confident. She wanted to reach out, trace the line of the scar, let her fingers linger on warm flesh.

She blinked, surprised by the train of her thoughts. Uncomfortable with them. Aside from her lapse of judgment two days after Christmas, Olivia had been separated from Ford for over a year. She'd been planning to sign divorce papers when she returned to Chicago for Martino's trial. In her mind, what they'd had was over.

She needed to keep it that way.

She rubbed the back of her neck, tried to refocus her thoughts. "Arguing isn't going to get us anywhere."

"That's why I'm leaving. Give me an hour. If I'm not back by then…" he hesitated, then continued. "Call the FBI. Ask for Jackson McGraw. He's the agent in charge of the Martino trial. Tell him you don't feel like the marshals can keep you safe."

"You think he'll be able to offer some other form of protection?"

"I don't know, and I'm praying that you won't have to find out. Stay here. I'll be back as soon as I can." He leaned down, brushing his lips over hers just as he had in her kitchen, the heat of his touch sweeping through Olivia, sending her back to other less complicated times. Times when she'd really believed that Ford would always love her.

"Stay here, Liv. Promise me."

"I promise." The words escaped before she realized they were forming, and Olivia bit her lip to keep from taking them back. What good would it do? If Ford came back, good. If not…she'd leave on her own. Going back to the FBI and marshals wasn't something she planned to do.

Ford walked outside, disappearing from view, and Olivia sat for several moments, her fingers pressing against her lips. He'd kissed her. Twice.

And he'd said he loved her.

It had been a long time since she'd heard those words.

Restless, she stood, pacing to windows that flanked either side of the door. Outside, darkness painted the street and houses in broad black strokes, hiding whatever danger might be hiding there. Olivia scanned the area, watching as a few people wandered past the church. Young. Laughing and jostling one another as they walked. Life went on the way it had before the fire had destroyed Olivia's home, before she'd nearly died, but she had changed. She'd realized that the responsibility for her safety lay in her own hands rather than the hands of others. If she were going to survive, if her baby was going to survive, she'd have to keep that in mind.

She sighed, letting her hand rest on her stomach. She wanted to open the door, run out into the night and disappear into the darkness. Wanted to forget about Vincent Martino, forget about the trial, forget everything but creating a good life for her child. She wanted to, but couldn't. Vincent Martino was a cold-blooded killer. Olivia had watched him shoot a rival crime boss. If Olivia didn't testify, he might go free. Free to kill again. That was something Olivia couldn't allow.

"Miss? Can I help you?" A woman asked, her voice coming behind Olivia.

Olivia jumped, her heart slamming against her ribs as she turned to face the woman. "No, I was just…"

What *was* she doing? Hiding from the federal government and hired assassins didn't seem like an answer she should give.

"I heard you come in several minutes ago, but I was on the phone with a parishioner. Couldn't get the poor old soul off the phone. You know how that is," the woman said, smiling from behind large, broad-rimmed glasses.

"Yes."

"I did finally manage to convince her that choir practice shouldn't be canceled just because she couldn't make it. And, now, I'll be happy to help you with whatever it is you need." Her smile continued as she drew closer, her gold-green eyes resting on Olivia's face, dropping to her clothes and then returning. "Are you all right?"

"Fine. I'm just waiting for a friend. I hope that's okay."

"Of course it is," she responded, her wiry gray hair bouncing as she cocked her head to the side. "I hope you don't think I'm being nosey, but it looks like you've been in an accident. Is there something I can do to help?"

An accident?

For a moment Olivia wasn't sure what the woman was talking about. Then it clicked. The fire. Heaven knew what she looked like after standing in the smoky kitchen and crawling across the floor. The rag she'd wrapped around her face had probably streaked whatever soot and grime had been there. She started to wipe at her cheeks, but stopped herself. The damage was already done and the mess she was in couldn't be hidden. She needed to answer the question in such a way that the woman didn't feel the need to call the police. "I appreciate the offer, but I'm fine. It's just…I was in a house fire."

"That explains all those sirens I heard. It

sounded like the entire fire department was racing through town."

"It was an extensive fire. I think my house is totally destroyed. The firefighters are still working to control the blaze, and I just couldn't bear to watch it burn. I started walking and found myself here. It seemed like the right place to stop." The words spewed out, and Olivia bit her lip to keep from saying more. Too much information, and she might give something away that she shouldn't.

"I'm glad you thought so. You've been through something terrible, but thank the good Lord you survived. Why don't you have a seat? I'll get you some hot, sweet tea. Is there someone you'd like me to call for you? A friend or family member who can take you in until your house is rebuilt? If not, I'm sure someone in our church can help you out."

"I've got my…" Husband. The word was on the tip of her tongue, but she refused to give it voice. She'd put Ford in a box after she'd left Chicago. A box she'd titled The Man I Used To Be Married To. Changing the title just might change how she saw him, and that could only lead to hurt. "Friend. He'll be here shortly."

"Good. I'd hate for you to be alone at a time like this. Especially in your condition."

"Condition?"

"You're not pregnant?"

Surprised, Olivia glanced down at her stomach. She'd noticed the slight pop to her belly. Now, in the course of several hours, two other people had commented on it. One of them was a complete stranger. How long would it take Ford to notice? "I didn't think it was that noticeable."

"I'm sure it's not, but I've got three daughters and nine grandkids. I can spot a pregnant woman a mile away. Now, how about I get you that tea?"

"That's okay. I'm fine. I'll just wait here until my friend comes if that's okay."

"Of course it is. I'll be in the office if you need anything."

"Thank you." Olivia smiled, but it fell away as soon as the woman disappeared into an office at the end of the hall.

In the two and a half months it had been since she'd taken the first pregnancy test and realized she was carrying Ford's child, she'd felt guilty for not letting him know. That guilt had been tempered by the reality of her situation. If she contacted him, there was every chance the Martinos would find her. It had been a valid excuse for keeping him in the dark, but there was no excuse now. She'd been found. Ford had reentered her life. Telling him about the baby was the only logical thing to do.

Except that Ford had made it very clear he didn't want children. Ever. They'd discussed it before their marriage and Olivia had brought it up several times after they'd said "I do," but Ford's stance on children hadn't wavered. They were too much work, too much mess and too time-consuming. He had other things he wanted to expend his energy on.

One thing, anyway.

His career. Building a real estate brokerage and a fortune.

Maybe telling him about the baby was the wrong thing to do. Despite his tender kisses and sweet words of love, Ford was more committed to his work than he was to anything else. A clean break, a new start, was what they both needed, and she was sure that Ford would be happy enough to go back to his busy schedule and workaholic ways once he was sure she was safe.

But could Olivia go on with her life knowing that she had kept something so important from him?

She rubbed the back of her neck as she stared out into the night. In a few months she'd turn thirty-three. An age when she'd thought she would have her life figured out. Instead she was more confused than ever.

A car pulled up in front the church, idled there for a moment and sped away. Olivia shrank back from the window, her heart beating wildly. Worrying about whether or not she should tell Ford

about the baby was a waste of energy. What she
should really be worrying about was getting out of
Pine Bluff alive.

*You shouldn't be worrying about anything. God
is in control. You just have to trust Him.*

The thought flitted through her mind, and she
tried to cling to it, believe it. But belief was as
elusive as a dream, and all she could do was pray
that whatever decision she made would be the right
one.

FOUR

A half hour passed. Then another. Olivia glanced at her watch for what seemed like the hundredth time and frowned. Ford had said to give him an hour. An hour had passed. Should she stay? Go?

She sidled up to the window and peered outside again. It would be easy to lose herself in the velvety darkness. To walk away from the church, the town and her problems. The trouble was, she couldn't walk far enough to escape the guilt she'd feel if she simply disappeared. Guilt for not doing her best to put a cold-blooded murderer behind bars, guilt for reneging on her agreement to testify, guilt for not letting Ford know the truth about the baby.

A few cars passed the church, and Olivia stiffened. Any one of them could be carrying Martino's men. She needed to make a decision about what to do, and she needed to make it quickly. Another car approached the church, stopping in front of the building. It had barely parked when the driver's door swung open and a dark figure jumped out. Olivia tumbled back, a scream hovering on her lips and then dying as she watched the shadowy form move toward the church. Tall and lanky with broad shoulders and a long, brisk stride, he could have been anyone, but Olivia knew him immediately. Ford.

Relieved, she pulled open the door, stepping aside as he rushed into the church. "What took you so long?"

"Paperwork. Come on. Let's get out of here," he said as he grabbed Olivia's hand and tugged her out the door.

"What's wrong?"

"Just a feeling."

"What kind of feeling?"

"The kind that's telling me if we don't get out of town soon, we won't get out at all." He opened the car door and urged Olivia inside, barely waiting for her to scoot into the seat before he slammed the door closed.

It took him just a few seconds to round the car and get in, but Olivia had already caught his anxiety. The hair on the back of her neck stood on end and fear roiled in her stomach. Despite the darkness, she felt exposed, as if a hundred eyes watched from the shadows.

Ford pulled away from the church, driving in the same steady, confident manner he always had. She'd admired that when they'd had to weave their way through Chicago traffic, but right now she'd rather he speed.

"Maybe you could drive faster," she muttered, scanning the dark street as he pulled onto Main Street and headed toward the edge of town.

"And risk being pulled over by the police?"

"I'd rather be pulled over by the police than found by the Martinos."

"I'd rather neither happen." He glanced into the rearview mirror, and Olivia shifted in her seat so she had a view of the road behind them. A few cars followed them past the town's limits and onto the highway, but none seemed in a hurry to catch up.

"Do you think anyone is following?" Olivia asked, unable to tamp down her anxiety. She'd been living on the edge for months, jumping at shadows, waking in the middle of the night sure she heard someone creeping through the house. Fear was insidious, and no matter how much she'd tried to believe that the FBI and the marshals were keeping her safe, there hadn't been a day since she'd seen Vincent Martino murder a man that she'd felt safe.

"I don't know." Ford's voice was tight, and Olivia shifted back around so she could study his face. He looked tense, the thin scar that cut across his cheek adding a dangerous edge to what had always been almost too-handsome features. Blond with striking blue eyes and a quick smile, he was the kind of guy who attracted women without effort. Olivia doubted the scar had changed that. Not that it mattered. Soon they'd be divorced, and Ford would be free to attract whomever he wanted.

"Ford, you shouldn't be here with me. You should be back in Chicago, running your business, making your deals. Going on with your life."

"Do you really think that would be a possibility, Livy? Do you really think I could just forget you and move on?"

"Isn't that what we planned to do? We agreed to separate, to try things on our own for a while."

"And we realized it didn't work."

"It was working just fine."

"You're saying you were happy to have me out of your life?" he asked as he took the ramp onto the interstate.

Olivia wanted to say yes. Not just say it, shout it. When she'd walked out of their Chicago penthouse, she'd been desperate to prove she could be happy without Ford, because being happy without him had seemed much better than being miserable with him. Being happy without him would have proven that she didn't need Ford. That her life could be fulfilling and wonderful without the only man she'd ever loved.

She frowned.

Only man she'd ever loved?

Maybe, but that didn't mean she couldn't love someone else. She just hadn't given herself a chance. Ford had bowled her over with his charm and intelligence, and she'd been drawn to his charismatic personality in the same way everyone else seemed to have been, but that didn't mean she couldn't love someone else if she chose to.

"I'll take your silence as a no, and assume you've been as unhappy with the separation as I've been," he said, breaking into her thoughts, but not sounding nearly as self-satisfied as she expected.

"Ending our marriage wasn't an easy thing to do."

"We didn't end it, Olivia. We're still married."

"Until we can sign the divorce papers," she said, knowing she sounded truculent and irritated. Ford had a way of doing that to her, his confidence only highlighting her own insecurities.

"If you still want a divorce after we get through Martino's trial, I'll give you one."

"But you think I won't want one."

"I *hope* you won't. I want another chance, Olivia. I've spent a lot of our marriage focusing on things that don't matter. I plan to spend the rest of it focusing on you."

They were sweet words. Words that she wished she could believe in, but she knew her husband. Whatever he was feeling would only last until the next big deal. Then, he'd get caught up in his work and forget that he planned to put her first.

It won't take the next big deal for that to happen. He'll turn tail and run as soon as he finds out about the baby.

The thought whispered through her mind, reminding her that she was keeping something very important from Ford. Something that would change the way he thought of their relationship and their future. Maybe he did think he'd be willing to devote more of himself to Olivia, but she was sure he'd be appalled at the thought of having to share his time and his love with a baby.

She had to tell him anyway. Putting it off wouldn't change anything. Ford had a right to know he'd fathered a child no matter how unhappy the news would make him.

She cleared her throat, tried to get the words out. "Ford, there's something I need to tell you."

"Go ahead. I'm listening." He glanced in her direction, offering a quick smile before turning his attention back to the road.

This was it. The opportunity she'd both longed for and dreaded since the day she'd found out she was pregnant.

Give me the words, Lord. Help me say what needs to be said without defensiveness.

"That night in December when you came to see me…" *Just say it!*

"I was an idiot, and I'm sorry. I should never have taken that phone call. No real estate deal is worth losing you over."

"It's not that…"

A shrill ring interrupted her words, and Ford pulled a cell phone from a clip on his belt, glanced at the caller ID and frowned. "It's the FBI."

"The FBI?" Olivia repeated, trying to switch gears from worrying about how to reveal the news of her pregnancy to worrying about why the FBI was calling Ford.

Not that there was any question about why. Olivia had only met with Special Agent Jackson McGraw twice, but it was enough to know that he was as determined and meticulous as Ford. He was trying to find Olivia, and he'd call until Ford answered, ask until he was given what he wanted.

"I'll call back later. What were you saying?" Ford slid the phone back onto his belt, apparently determined to let Olivia finish what she was saying. It was a first. Over the course of their marriage, she'd been interrupted by phone calls so many times she'd given up on having meaningful conversations with Ford.

"You pick now to ignore a phone call?" she asked, not sure if she should be flattered or appalled.

"I promised myself that if I found you, I'd do what I should have been doing for the past ten years—put you first."

"I appreciate the thought, but putting me ahead of work is one thing. Putting me ahead of a phone call from the FBI is something else. You'd better call back and see what they want."

"I already know what they want. They want me to tell them where we are so they can get you back into the witness Protection Program."

"They're the FBI, Ford. You can't ignore them."

"I just did."

"You're being unreasonable."

"I'm being cautious. Who's to say James was right? Maybe the leak isn't in the marshals? Maybe it's in the FBI."

"A leak doesn't mean everyone in the FBI and U.S. Marshals is crooked."

"You're right, but I've had federal agents following me off and on since I flew into Billings a few weeks ago. It's possible the marshals let them know I'd arrived in Pine Bluff and that I was getting close to finding you."

"You're sounding a little paranoid, Ford."

"I'm sounding like a guy who's been searching

for his wife for months. A guy who will do whatever it takes to keep her safe."

The phone rang again, and Ford frowned, pulling it out and glancing at the caller ID again. "They're persistent. That's for sure."

"They can probably trace us using the signal from your cell phone, so you may as well see what they want." And while he was talking, Olivia would plan another way of breaking the news about the baby. So far, she'd botched the job, but eventually she'd have to get the words out.

"All right, but we'll pick up our conversation as soon as I finish." He pressed the phone to his ear, nearly barking a greeting.

Olivia stared out the window, watching as the dark landscape flew past. She'd driven along this road a month ago, heading from Billings to Pine Bluff, not even knowing her destination. The female marshal who'd sat in the backseat of the car with her had made small talk, but Olivia remembered little of the conversation. Her mind had been on the two witnesses who'd been murdered and on her own mortality. Dying wasn't something she wanted to do, but she wasn't afraid of doing it. What she feared was never having a chance to experience motherhood, to hold her infant, play with her baby, watch her toddler explore the world. She wanted those things with a desperation she hadn't thought possible.

"What are you talking about, McGraw?" The volume of Ford's voice rose, and Olivia's gaze jumped to him.

He shot a look in her direction, something akin to horror in his eyes.

Had someone else been murdered? Another witness?

"Give me a half hour. I'll call you and let you know what we're going to do." Ford tossed the phone onto the console.

"What's going on?"

"Special Agent McGraw wants you back under marshal protection."

"That's not news."

"No. It isn't." His voice was tight with an emotion Olivia couldn't quite put her finger on. Anger? Frustration? Fear?

She didn't know, but her own anxiety rose. "What's going on, Ford?"

He shook his head, his jaw clenched as he took an exit ramp and pulled into a rest stop. They were the only car in the lot, but Ford pulled into a spot far from the building and shrouded in darkness.

Obviously, there was more going on than what he'd said. Olivia braced herself as he turned off the car and shifted in his seat, sure that whatever he had to say wouldn't be pleasant. Silence pressed in around them, carrying its own rhythm and pulse.

Olivia could feel it seep into her pores, whisper in her ear. Something was wrong.

Ford's eyes were black as pitch, glowing darkly in the dim light cast from a distant streetlight. He studied Olivia's face, his gaze dropping from her eyes, to her cheeks, then to her lips, the intensity of his gaze a heated caress that left her breathless.

Finally, his gaze dropped away and landed squarely on her stomach. "Special Agent McGraw had some interesting things to say."

"He did?" Olivia asked, knowing exactly what those interesting things must have been.

"He said it's imperative that we get you back under federal protection. He also said it's not just your life we've got to worry about." He lifted his eyes, looked into her face, his expression unreadable. The sick hollow feeling Olivia had had for months gnawed at her stomach, but she wouldn't deny what she knew he was asking, wouldn't put off the inevitable any longer.

She took a deep breath, trying to fill her lungs with air and her heart with confidence. No matter what Ford's response, she was having a baby. Finally, after years of dreaming and wishing and praying, she would be a mother with or without Ford's presence in her life.

She straightened her spine, looked into Ford's eyes and told him the news that had filled her with joy. The news she knew would fill him with horror. "That's what I was trying to tell you, Ford. I'm pregnant."

FIVE

Pregnant?!

Ford tried to wrap his mind around the word, tried to make sense of it.

"What did you say?" he asked by rote, knowing that he hadn't been mistaken in what he'd heard.

"I'm pregnant," Olivia repeated, her face pale in the dim light, her eyes wide and filled with apprehension.

"Whose is it?" The question popped out without thought, and Olivia stiffened, her lips tightening into a thin line. She didn't speak, just stared him down, daring him to repeat the question.

He didn't.

He knew the answer. Had known it before he'd even asked the question. Olivia wasn't the kind for one-night stands. Though he'd refused to attend service with her, Olivia had always believed that Sunday mornings were for church. It wasn't just the place, though, that drew her there. It was a deep-seated faith that he'd only just recently begun to understand. That faith had given Olivia a strong sense of morality and belief in the sanctity of marriage. She'd made that clear when they were dating, told him that she planned to have only one great love. He'd felt privileged to be the one.

Unfortunately, he'd been too much of a fool to act like it.

"I'm sorry." He issued the apology through the hard, tight knot in his throat. Olivia was pregnant with his child. He'd spent thirty-four years saying he'd never be a father. Now the choice had been taken from him. Whether he liked it or not, he was going to have an innocent life in his hands.

And he'd ruin it just as his father had. Just as his grandfather had.

"You should be," Olivia bit out, turning away to stare out her window, arms hugged tight around her waist. Her shoulders and back were as slender as ever, the line of her jaw unchanged. If anything, she seemed more slender than when he'd last seen her, but, then, he hadn't gotten a good look at her stomach, had had no reason to study it. Now he wished he'd looked. Maybe he would have noticed the pregnancy and been spared the surprise. At least then he could have thought through what he wanted to say and how he wanted to say it. The last thing Olivia needed was to be hurt by his careless words.

"I'd ask you how it happened, but I guess I know."

"The pregnancy doesn't change anything, Ford. You're under no obligation to me or my child."

"*Yours?* It's *our* child."

"A child you don't want."

It was the truth. He couldn't deny it. He'd been born from three generations of bad fathering. His great-grandfather was an alcoholic who abused his children. His grandfather abandoned his wife and son. Ford's father had been no better. By the time Ford was twelve, his dad was gone, leaving his children with a drug-addicted mother who was incapable of caring for her family.

Ford had no plans to continue that legacy.

Yet it seemed he was about to.

"I've never made my feelings about having kids a secret."

"And I never would have purposely gotten pregnant no matter how much I wanted a child. But it happened, and I'd be lying if I said I wasn't happy about it," she said, not turning away from the window.

"We'll work it out." It was all he could manage, and it wasn't enough. He knew it, but could offer nothing else.

"*We* won't do anything, Ford. You'll drive me to wherever the FBI wants me to go. Then you'll go back to Chicago and get on with your life."

"You know that's not how it's going to work."

"Why not? During our marriage, you made it more than clear you didn't want children. You made it pretty clear you didn't want me, either. As scary as the past few months have been, they've taught me something, Ford. I'm just fine on my own. I don't need you or our marriage to be happy."

"This isn't about either of us being happy. This is about our child needing a father," he said, gritting his teeth to keep from saying more.

"There are plenty of children being raised without fathers. My baby will be just fine."

"*Our* baby."

She whipped around, her eyes flashing with anger. *"You don't want this baby."*

"The baby is coming whether I want it or not. And I plan to take responsibility for it."

"It? It! We're talking about a child," Olivia responded, her words tight and controlled as if she were afraid to let loose the emotions Ford could see clearly in her eyes. Anger. Frustration. Fear.

What did she think he would do? Demand custody of the baby? Demand she end the pregnancy?

The shrill ring of his cell phone broke through the tension in the car, and Ford grabbed it, happy for an excuse not to ask the questions spinning through his mind. "Jensen here."

"Special Agent McGraw. Did you two come to an agreement about allowing us to bring you into headquarters?"

"We're discussing it."

"Discuss it quickly, because the longer you're out on your own, the more likely it is Martino's men will find you."

"Who's to say they won't find us anyway? They did show up in Pine Bluff tonight. Or have you forgotten that?" He asked, his gaze still on Olivia. She'd turned to stare out the window again, her hair falling forward to hide her face. Was she crying?

"We've been working closely with the marshals to make sure that doesn't happen again."

"Were you working closely when they found two other witnesses and murdered them?"

McGraw's silence conveyed plenty. Irritation for one. Lack of answers for another. Ford waited him out. He'd been dealing with Special Agent Jackson McGraw since the day Olivia had called to tell him that she'd witnessed a murder and was going into the witness protection program. McGraw was professional and thorough, and he wasn't one to speak without thinking through what he was going to say.

"Look, Ford, I know you're worried about your wife and your child. I don't blame you, but we can offer Olivia the kind of protection she needs to stay safe until the trial. I think you'll agree that you can't."

"I can offer her anonymity."

"Are you saying we can't keep her hidden?"

"I'm saying what I said before, someone found her today. That makes me doubt your ability to keep her hidden until the trial."

"*You* found her today. We've got every reason to believe that's what led the Martinos to her."

"We can argue all night, McGraw, but facts are facts. No one followed me to Pine Bluff. I'm sure of it. That means that someone leaked Olivia's whereabouts to the Martino's."

"You're making some major assumptions, Ford. If you were able to find her without our help, someone else could have, too."

"Maybe." And if not for Marshal James's warning about a leak in the marshals, Ford might have been willing to believe that's exactly what happened.

"Look, this isn't something I wanted Olivia to worry about, but it's something you need to know. Word on the street has it that the price on Olivia's head has increased. Five hundred thousand dollars to anyone who can get rid of her before the trial."

"How likely is that information to be true?" Ford met Olivia's eyes, wondered if she'd heard McGraw's words.

"Very. She might be a moving target, but she's still a target. The sooner you get her back under our protection, the better."

"Yours or the marshals?" No way would Ford bring her back into the marshal's care.

"Both. I've got a task force assembled that is working hard to keep Olivia safe. She'll be a lot safer with us than she will be out on the street."

Ford glanced at Olivia again. She sat tense and still, soft strands of dark hair falling over her shoulders. How many times had he watched her while she slept, traced her delicate features with his eyes? Wondered if he could make what they had last?

He couldn't let her be hurt.

Wouldn't let her be hurt. Not if he could help it.

The question was, would it safer to go it alone, or to bring in the FBI?

Ford had never been much for praying or for faith. He'd learned early that the only one he could count on was himself, but lately he'd begun to wonder if unseen hands were guiding him. If perhaps God wasn't nearly as distant as Ford had always believed. He should have died when Martino's men had broken into his home and questioned him about Olivia. He'd thought he *would* die. As darkness closed in, he'd done what he hadn't in years—called out to God, begged for more time. A second chance.

He'd been given it.

He couldn't mess it up.

What do I do, Lord? How do I keep her safe?

"You still there, Ford?"

"I'm here."

"I need a decision, man. You know that, right?"

"Yeah. Olivia and I will fly into Chicago. I'll call you when we get there. You can meet us at the airport or we can drive to your office."

"That's too dangerous. Martino's men might have the airport staked out. Here's what I think we need to do. You drive into Billings. Go straight to our district office. We'll put both of you under twenty-four-hour guard and provide an armed escort back to Chicago. I'm not going to inform anyone of these plans. You shouldn't, either. No check-ins with the marshals and no phone calls to anyone. We can only keep you safe if we limit the number of people who know you're coming into FBI protection."

"Understood."

"Do you have an ETA for Billings?"

"Three hours."

"Call me when you get into town."

"Will do."

"I don't need to remind you of how dangerous the Martinos are. Be careful, and watch your back." McGraw hung up, and Ford slid the cell phone back into its case. McGraw was right, he didn't need a reminder of how dangerous Martino's men were. He wore the evidence of their brutality on his face and ribs, the scars still raw and tender. The thought of Olivia suffering a similar fate, suffering a worse one, filled him rage and fear.

He turned the ignition, the sound of the engine filling the silence.

Olivia turned, her face pale and drawn, her eyes deeply shadowed. "You could have asked me what I wanted to do, Ford."

"I can't risk your life, Olivia. I can't risk the baby's."

"You still could have asked," Olivia said, sounding more resigned than anything.

"So, I'm asking. Do you want to go ahead with this? Do you want us to turn ourselves in to the FBI? Or would you rather keep running and hope we escape?"

"What I want is to be back in my house in Chicago two days after Christmas. What I want is to send you away instead of letting you in."

"Thereby keeping everything that's happened in the past few months from happening?"

She shrugged a slender shoulder. "I'd like to say that, but even if I could go back and change things, I wouldn't."

Because of the baby.

She didn't say the words, but Ford heard them. From the time they'd met, he'd looked at Olivia and seen a woman who would make a great mother. Caring and compassionate, she had a natural affinity for children. During the first years of their marriage, she'd volunteered at the local Y, teaching ballet classes and nurturing the children in her class with selfless abandon. As his real estate business had grown, she'd given up volunteer work to help him run his office. He'd never felt guilty about that, but he should have.

There were so many things about their marriage Ford regretted, so many opportunities he'd missed, but there was one thing he couldn't regret, and that was his unwillingness to have children. No matter how much he loved Olivia, having a child with her had never been an option.

But now it was a reality.

And he still wasn't sure what he thought about that.

He pulled away from the rest area, the silence between Olivia and him settling as thick and deep as the night. Midnight blue, the sky seemed alive with starlight and shadows. In the distance, towering mountains were a deeper black against the sky. The road stretched out for miles, empty of cars or light. Billings was two hundred miles away. An easy drive if they didn't run into trouble. Ford needed to focus on making sure they didn't. Anything else would have to wait.

SIX

Olivia had never minded silence, but the silence in Ford's car was thick and heavy with unspoken words. Olivia wanted to break it, but could think of nothing to say. She wouldn't apologize for being pregnant. Couldn't deny the joy it brought her. Refused to beg Ford to feel the same.

After all, she already knew how he felt. The same way her parents had felt about children—they were too noisy, too disruptive, too much trouble. As the only child of a heart surgeon and an oncologist, Olivia had lived a childhood filled with things and lacking in love. Her parents had been too busy pursuing careers to spend time with their daughter. If they had loved her, that might have been okay.

They'd tolerated her.

That's the way Olivia had always felt. When she'd called them to say she was going into witness protection and that they'd probably never see her again, her mother had simply wished her luck. Her father had told her it was for the best that she cooperate with the FBI. She hadn't been surprised or even hurt. She'd given up on having a relationship with her parents long ago. But living with her parents, understanding what it meant to be an unwanted child, had made her realize how much children craved their parents' affection. It had been that more than anything else that had kept Olivia from pressing Ford for children during their marriage.

And now she was pregnant with a child Ford didn't want. Hot tears filled her eyes and clogged her throat, but she forced them back.

The baby she was carrying could never know that its father didn't want him or her. No matter how much it hurt to say goodbye to Ford, no matter how much she longed to believe Ford when he said he wanted to make their marriage work, the baby had to be her first priority.

"Ford, I know that my pregnancy is a shock," she said, breaking the silence, filling it with words that could do nothing to change the situation.

"That's putting it mildly," he muttered in reply, his hands fisted around the steering wheel, his tension radiating out until Olivia was sure the air was vibrating with it.

"I was shocked, too, when I found out. At first,

I was sure there was some kind of mistake. I mean, what are the chances?" She laughed hollowly, wishing she were a better actress. If she wanted Ford to think she was okay and that the pregnancy hadn't shaken her, she needed to sound more light-hearted than upset.

"Yeah. I was thinking the same."

There was an edge to his voice that Olivia didn't like, and she clenched her teeth to keep from lashing out. "Are you implying that I planned to get pregnant? That somehow I duped you into becoming a father?"

"I'm not implying anything. I'm *saying* that you always wanted kids. Now you've gotten what you wanted."

"I didn't come looking for you that night, Ford. You came looking for me," she said, sick with regret and anger.

"I know that, Livy. I know."

"And now you regret it."

"I regret that I can't be happy about this baby. I regret that I'll be a failure as a father, but I don't regret what happened that night. I don't regret that we're together now."

"How can we be together when you don't want our child? Don't you see? It won't work, Ford. You'll resent the time I spend with the baby, and I'll resent you for it. And we'll be right back where we've always been. Going our own ways. Doing our own things."

"I went my own way, Liv. You were always right there with me, coming along for the ride. I know that, and I'm not doing it again. You're pregnant. I'll deal with it."

"I don't want you to deal with it. I want…" Her voice broke, and she stopped.

"You want me to be happy. I'm not. I'm not the kind of guy who wants to hang around the house changing diapers and burping babies, and I know that will hurt you. Hurt our child."

"How can you know that until you've tried?"

"Fatherhood isn't something you try. It's something you do, and since I learned how to be a father from the worst, I'm sure I'll fail at it completely."

"It's not like my parents were peaches."

"But you're a different kind of person than I am, Liv. You've got what it takes to be a mother. What I've got is selfish ambition and a bucket load of drive. It takes a lot more than that to raise a kid right." Ford's response held no heat. If anything he sounded tired.

That was something Olivia understood. She was tired, too. Tired of running. Tired of fighting. Tired of pretending that everything was okay when the world was falling apart around her. "I'm scared, too, Ford. I want this baby to have so much more than what either of us had, and sometimes I'm so worried that I won't be able to provide it."

"So we're going to have a baby that neither of us knows how to parent. And you're happy about that?" he snapped, and then took a deep breath. "I'm sorry. That didn't come out right."

"Didn't it?" Olivia turned and stared out the window, wanting to end the conversation, return to the comforting rhythm of silence. That had been how she'd spent the months before they'd separated. Silent in the face of Ford's rejection. No more tears when he refused to go on vacations she'd planned for them. No more arguments when he'd said he had to work late again.

"No, it didn't. Hearing that you're pregnant was a shock, Livy. I'm sure you realize that. I'm not thinking straight." He paused, but Olivia didn't speak. Ford had always been good at manipulating conversations. No matter what Olivia said, he could easily twist it to suit his purposes. Better to keep silent and let him explain exactly why having a baby wasn't a good idea.

Then she could tell him how much she didn't care what he thought. The baby was coming. He'd just have to deal with it.

"Look, I've been on the road for the better part of three months. I'm exhausted, and I'm in no position to discuss the baby rationally. What I'm worried about right now is getting you to Billings and Special Agent McGraw. After that, we'll have time to discuss how we're going to handle being parents."

Okay. That wasn't what Olivia expected. She'd been sure he would list the top ten reasons they couldn't be having a baby. Maybe tell her how a child would ruin their quality of life. "How we're going to handle being parents?"

"Yeah. The baby *is* coming, after all. Whether we're happy about it or not."

"I *am* happy," she said, the tears she'd been fighting burning at the back of her throat again.

Ford's hand dropped onto her knee, and he squeezed gently. "I know, babe, and I'm happy for you."

Happy for *her?*

Did he really think that was enough?

"Ford—"

He shot a look in her direction, but didn't flash the quick, charming smile that had captured her heart the day they'd met. "I'm not the same person I was in December, Livy. You may as well know that now. I've had to take a hard look at my life, and I don't much like what I've seen. I'm trying to change, but changing is a process. It doesn't happen overnight."

"I know."

"Do you? Because I'm asking you to give me time. To trust that I mean what I'm saying."

"What are you saying, Ford?"

"That you're not going to spend another anniversary or birthday alone. That you'll never wait at a restaurant wondering if I'll show up again. That you can count on me."

"And the baby?"

"Like I said, we'll talk about that after I get you to Billings."

Olivia wanted to push for more, but didn't. She'd spent a lot of time praying about sharing the news about the baby with Ford. She'd always known that if it were going to happen, God would have to orchestrate it. He had. Now Olivia would have to wait and see what else He had planned, because as much as Olivia wanted to believe Ford had changed, she couldn't.

Over the course of their marriage, he'd said he was sorry too many times to count. But words were a dime a dozen, and Olivia had stopped believing in them years ago. "When is Special Agent McGraw expecting us in Billings?"

"I told him three hours. Hopefully, it won't take us much longer than that." Ford seemed relieved to change the subject, his tight expression easing. He looked harder than he had during their marriage. Maybe it was the scar or maybe it was what he'd been through. Had the Martinos attacked him? He hadn't denied it. Hadn't confirmed it. Olivia needed to ask, but wasn't sure she wanted to know the answer. She'd wait for another time. A time when hearing that she'd been the reason he was hurt wouldn't bring on the tears that threatened.

"Does Marshal McGraw know we're headed back to Billings?" she asked, knowing she was a coward, and not caring.

"I'm not sure. Jackson mentioned a special task force. If Marshal McGraw is on it, he'll know. Otherwise, he's probably still in the dark."

"Did Jackson mention the leak?"

"No, but that's not surprising. I doubt the FBI and U.S. Marshals want the public knowing they've got that kind of trouble."

"Two women have already died. You'd think people would be getting a clue."

"If you hadn't been in the Witness Protection Program, I probably wouldn't have had any knowledge about the two women who were killed in Montana."

"I'm surprised you heard about them, anyway. It seems like the story of two women being murdered several states away wouldn't make the Chicago news."

"I would have read the story no matter what

newspaper it was in. I hired half a dozen private detectives after you called me. They were scouring newspapers, watching airports and trying to get a feel for where the marshals might have taken you."

"Still, it's a miracle you found me. This is a big country. It's easy to get lost in it."

"Yeah, that's what Special Agent McGraw kept telling me. He said that searching for you was a waste of time and money. That you'd show up at Vincent Martino's trial and that I could speak to you then."

"It's true. You could have waited until then. It would have saved you a lot of effort."

"No, I couldn't have waited. Martino plays for keeps, Olivia. You know that. I was worried that one of his men would find you and that you'd have to face that alone."

"I wouldn't have been alone. The marshals have been providing protection."

"Which brings us right back to where we started. The marshals were providing protection for both the women who were killed. I wasn't going to wait to see if they got it right with you."

"The marshals are good people. They know what they're doing."

"You don't have to tell me that. I saw the way they worked tonight. They'd have given their lives to protect you, but that doesn't mean one of their numbers hasn't gone bad. Both the women who were killed were in Montana. It seems to me, and it seemed to the private investigator that brought me the article, that the Martinos' hitmen were shooting at any target that looked promising, not caring too much if they got the right one."

"You're making a lot of assumptions, Ford. We don't even know if they were murdered by the same person."

"No? Did you realize that both victims had black marks on their hands?"

"No."

"I spoke with some officers who worked the cases. They offered the information when they found out who I was."

"The Montana police were impressed by the fact that you're a Chicago real estate magnate?" No way. There had to be another reason.

"They were impressed that I survived an attack by Martino's men. They wanted to help me find you because they were as worried as I was that you'd end up like the other two women."

"Whoever murdered those women wasn't necessarily gunning for me," Olivia said, her voice faint even to her own ears. The thought of Ford being attacked by Martino's goons sickened her. Her stomach hadn't been quite right since she'd gotten pregnant. Would she have to ask him to pull over?

"No, but why take chances? Jackson McGraw is right to keep your Billings return under wraps."

"I know," she said, her gaze on the scar. Purplish-red and raised, it still looked raw.

"What happened, Ford?"

"Happened?"

She touched the scar, her fingers tracing the line of it down his cheek. "What did Martino's men do to you?"

"They paid me a visit the day after you went into witness protection. They thought I might know where you were."

"I'm so sorry." Sorry he'd been hurt. Sorry that she was the reason. She should have known Ford would be in danger. She'd seen how easily Martino pulled the trigger on his rival. Seen how nonchalant he was as he'd tucked the gun back under his jacket. As if he hadn't just put a hole through another man's head, hadn't used his foot to nudge the body into the river.

"It wasn't your fault, Olivia."

"It feels like it was."

"Because you think if you try hard enough, if you work hard enough, you can keep bad things from happening to the people you care about. You can't. Only God has that power."

"God? Since when did you start talking about God?" Olivia asked, shocked by Ford's words.

He'd refused to attend church with her during their marriage. When pushed, he'd said he believed in God, but he also believed that church was for people who had nothing better to do with their time.

"Since I was staring down the barrel of a gun and realizing I might be breathing my last," he said, fingering the scar.

The sick, churning feeling in the pit of Olivia's stomach intensified.

"Ford—"

"Like I said, what happened wasn't your fault. Rehashing it won't change it. So, let's drop the subject and move on."

Maybe she *should* drop the subject.

Maybe she *should* move on.

But she couldn't. She reached out, almost touched the scar again, realized what she was doing and let her hand fall away. "Were you shot?"

"I knocked the gunman's hand to the side. The bullet that was meant for my face just grazed my cheek."

"Just? You could have died."

"But I didn't. And I realized something important from the experience. Life is finite. We're never guaranteed a second chance. I've got this one, Olivia. And I'm not going to mess it up. The FBI wanted me to go into witness protection after the attack, but there was no way I could do that. Not until I knew you were okay."

"I wish you'd done what they wanted."

"Do you?" He glanced her way, met her eyes for one brief, heated moment.

"I…don't know." It was as much of the truth as she could give. As much as she could admit to herself or to Ford.

"That's more than I'd hoped for. See, being here with you, it's not just about keeping you safe. It's about love. Whether you believe it or not, whether I showed it or not during our marriage. I do love you, Liv. I always have. I always will."

What could she say to that?

Sorry, Ford, I don't believe you?

Or, *I love you, too, Ford, and I desperately want to believe we'll spend the rest of our lives together?*

She was confused. Thrown into a situation she hadn't expected, going by instinct, and instinct said the only person she could trust was herself.

And God.

He was the unseen hand that had led her to safety the night she'd seen Vincent Martino murder a man. He was the silent whisper late at night, telling her that everything would be okay.

When all else failed, when the world seemed to be falling apart, God was there. Circumstances changed, but He did not. That was the one thing that Olivia could count on, and it was enough.

She shifted in her seat, leaning her head back and staring up at the ceiling, listening to the silence and the quiet beat of her heart. Praying for the baby she carried. Praying for Ford. And praying that she would be strong enough to face whatever the next few weeks and months brought.

SEVEN

Olivia was asleep when Ford drove into Billings. One arm under her head, she rested against the door, her dark hair lying silky and thick against her shoulder and arm. She looked delicate and young, her smooth complexion and unlined skin pale in the light from the dashboard. If he looked closely enough, would he notice a slight swelling of her abdomen? Some other telltale sign of her pregnancy?

A baby.

His baby.

Ford still couldn't quite believe it.

Believe it or not, you're going to be a father.

Ford frowned, pulling out his cell phone, dialing Special Agent McGraw's number and waiting impatiently while it rang several times. Finally, McGraw answered.

"McGraw here."

"It's Ford Jensen. We've just hit Billings."

"Good. I've got a team lined up to offer twenty-four hour protection at a safe house in the area."

"You're not going to move us to a new location?"

"The team discussed it, but we think the Martinos will be expecting that. What they won't expect is for us to keep Olivia in Montana."

"You *hope* that's not what they'll expect."

"It's more than a hope or we'd be moving you. We've handpicked a few marshals—"

"I thought you said we were keeping them out of this."

"I said, only men and women who were part of the task force would have knowledge of Ms. Jarrod's whereabouts. There are marshals and FBI agents working on that team, and I trust every one of them," Jackson said, sounding as on edge as Ford felt.

"It's nearly one in the morning, and I've been driving three hours straight, so I guess I'll have to take your word on that. Where do you want me to go?"

"Holy Cross Hospital. It's on the south side of town. We've got some men waiting there."

"You want to know what kind of car I'm driving."

"We already do. When you drive into the parking lot, pull around to the emergency room entrance. Stay in the car until one of my men approaches."

"You're good at issuing orders, McGraw."

"I hope you're good at following them. Our men are wearing bulletproof gear. You're not, and neither is Olivia."

"Understood."

"Good. You have a GPS system in that car?"

"Yes."

"Here's the address." He rattled off the information, and Ford typed the information into the GPS system.

"Got it."

"How far out are you?"

"Just a few minutes. The streets are empty, so we should be able to get there quickly."

"I'll let my men know. Be careful, Jensen."

"I have been." Ford hung up, clipping the phone back to his belt.

"Was that Special Agent McGraw?" Olivia straightened in her seat, her face still soft with sleep.

"Yes. We're going to meet some of his people at a hospital in the area. They'll escort us to a safe house. We'll stay there until the trial."

"Three weeks in a safe house? That sounds like fun."

"More fun than dying, anyway."

"You've got a point. Sorry I fell asleep. I've been exhausted for weeks. I guess the baby is taking more than his fair share of my energy," she said casually, as if talking about the baby were no big deal.

"It's a boy?"

"There's a fifty-fifty chance it is."

And a fifty-fifty shot that it would be a girl. Would she look like Olivia? Dark hair. Sweet smile and dancing feet. For a moment, Ford allowed himself to imagine a child just like that, twirling in summer-green grass. He shoved the image away. "Do you plan to find out before it's born?"

"I haven't decided yet, and please stop calling him 'it.'"

He nodded, unwilling to say anything more, the same uncomfortable, sick feeling he had every time he thought of being a father churning in his stomach.

"Where's the hospital?" Olivia asked, changing the subject.

"Not far. You can see our progress on the map here." He pointed to the GPS system.

"I've always wanted to try one of these. I just never had any reason," Olivia said, leaning forward to get a better look, her arm brushing against his. Heat shot through Ford at the contact, filling him with memories and longing. He tamped both down, focusing instead on the dark road that stretched ahead.

Houses lined the street, bunched together in clusters. A church sat on a corner lot, its siding pale gray in the moonlight. Ford was sure he'd seen the exact same scene during the time he'd spent crisscrossing Billings. After nearly three weeks, every street corner, every house looked the same as the last, and he'd been ready to leave Billings, head to another state. He'd about given up hope of finding Olivia, had been ready to head out of town, when he'd run into a woman who'd recognized Olivia's picture. She hadn't been able to tell Ford much. Just that Olivia had been working at a local diner and that she'd left Billings, but it had been enough to keep him searching.

The GPS announced an approaching exit, and Ford took it, merging onto a two-lane highway, then turning into the hospital parking lot. He knew what he was supposed to do—drive to the emergency room entrance, wait for McGraw's men to make themselves known, but trusting Olivia's life to others wasn't something he was happy about doing. Especially when he wasn't sure how trust-worthy those people were.

"What now?" Olivia asked, as he idled near the parking lot entrance.

"I guess we go meet McGraw's men."

"You don't sound happy about it."

"I'm not, but I'm not sure we have any choice."

"I thought we'd already decided this was the best option?" As always, Olivia was reasonable and calm, but Ford could sense the anxiety in her words. Now wasn't the time to let her know how worried *he* was or how much he wondered if turning themselves over to the FBI was the right thing to do. They were committed to the plan, and adding extra stress to Olivia's life wasn't something Ford wanted to do.

"We did," he said, pulling through the hospital parking lot, the hair on the back of his neck standing on end. They were being watched. He was sure of it. He just hoped the people watching were the good guys.

"Did Special Agent McGraw say who was going to meet us?" Olivia asked, and Ford was sure he could hear the fear in her voice. That couldn't be good for the baby. Weren't pregnant women supposed to avoid extreme stress?

He frowned. He'd planned to avoid thinking about the baby until after the trial. Seemed his mind had other ideas. "No. Just that we'd be met by some of his people."

"Maybe Micah will be here. He and Special Agent McGraw are brothers, you know," she said almost absently, and Ford knew she was as busy scanning the parking lot as he was.

"I'd wondered."

"They are. I think Jackson is older, but I only saw him twice, and it's hard to remember exactly what he looked like. I do know that he seemed like a really kind man."

"Jackson McGraw, kind?"

"Yes, why?"

"He seemed more obstinate and annoying than kind when I met him," Ford responded. Though he couldn't say Jackson McGraw had been rude or unkind. It was more that he'd been determined to discourage Ford from going after Olivia. It hadn't worked because Ford was just as obstinate and determined as the FBI agent.

Ford followed the emergency room signs to the back of the building. The area was quiet. A few cars were parked in the lot, but they were far enough out that Ford couldn't see if anyone was in them. He pulled up behind a car that idled in the drop-off area, his pulse racing with nerves. Anyone could hop out of the idling vehicle. Good guy. Bad guy. And the unknown filled him with the kind of stone-cold fear he'd only ever felt once before.

What he needed was a weapon. A gun would work. It had been years since he's served in the marines, but he figured he could still hit a target if he needed to. Too bad he hadn't thought of that before he'd found Olivia. Weaponless, he wasn't going to stand much of a chance against armed men.

His cell phone rang, and Olivia jumped, screaming loudly enough to nearly break Ford's eardrums. He put a hand on her shoulder, trying to convey confidence as he lifted the phone to his ear. From the look of stark terror in her face, his efforts weren't paying off.

"Hello?"

"Ford? Jackson McGraw here. I've got two marshals and an agent moving toward you. Two men. One woman. Look out your back window. You should see them."

Ford shifted so he could do as he'd been asked. Just as Jackson said, three figures were moving toward the car. He couldn't tell their gender, but he was sure they were McGraw's people. "I see them."

"Good. Stay put until they're at the car. They'll escort you to your ride. We've got a few other people guarding the perimeter of the parking lot, so your safety is assured."

Just like Olivia's safety had been assured in Pine Bluff?

Ford didn't ask. No sense pouring salt on an open wound, and there was no sense needling a man who was obviously doing the best he could to keep Olivia safe. The problem was, Ford wasn't sure McGraw's best was going to be good enough. He wasn't sure anyone's best would be.

As Ford watched, one of the figures separated from the others, walked to Ford's side of the car and gestured for him to open the door.

Medium height and build, with sandy blond hair, he leaned into the open door, shooting a look at Olivia before focusing on Ford. "Mr. Jensen?"

"That's right."

"Marshal Anderson Lawrence," he said, offering a quick, hard handshake.

"Nice to meet you."

"Likewise. We're going to get into the car in front of yours. I'll escort you there."

"What about Olivia?"

"She'll be in the same car, but we'll wait until you're safely inside the vehicle before we move her."

Ford wanted to argue, but it would be a waste of time. The marshals had their methods, and they weren't going to change for him. He met Olivia's eyes. "Are you okay with that?"

"I'll be fine," she said, smiling the same sweet smile she'd offered the first day they'd met. Ford wanted to pull her close, press a kiss to her lips, tell her how much he loved her smile. How much he loved her.

"Ready, Mr. Jenson?" Marshal Lawrence's voice

held a note of impatience that Ford didn't miss and that he didn't appreciate. Unfortunately, he wasn't the one calling the shots. He leaned forward, letting his lips brush Olivia's for just a moment before he pulled away and got out of the car.

Cool night air enveloped him as he hurried to the waiting vehicle, and Ford inhaled deeply, trying to slow his rapid pulse. As far as he could tell there was no immediate danger, but his body hummed with awareness, his mind screamed a warning. Had this been the way Olivia had felt every moment of the past months? Had fear kept her heart beating rapidly, her ears straining for signs of danger?

He should have been there for her.

"Get in and slide across, Mr. Jensen," Marshal Lawrence said as he pulled open the back door of an idling Cadillac.

Ford gritted his teeth to keep from telling the marshal that he'd do what he wanted when he wanted. In his day-to-day life, Ford was the boss. He told his employees what to do and they did it. Not having control wasn't something he was used to, and it wasn't something he liked.

He got in the car anyway, sliding over to the far door as Marshal Lawrence walked away.

"How was the trip from Pine Bluff?" A man in the driver's seat asked, as if Ford and Olivia had been on a scenic jaunt rather than running for their lives.

"We didn't run into trouble if that's what you're asking," Ford replied, not bothering to turn his attention from the open door. How long did it take for three federal officers to get a woman from one car to another?

"Good. We didn't think you'd been followed out of town, but we weren't sure. I'm Marshal Micah McGraw, by the way."

McGraw?

Jackson McGraw's brother, and the marshal Olivia was on a first name basis with. Ford would have given the guy a once-over if he hadn't been so focused on the well-lit area outside of the car. Olivia would make an easy target as she got into the car. He hoped the marshals had thought that through.

"Don't worry. The team is just waiting for an all clear before they get Olivia out of the car," Micah said, as if he'd read Ford's thoughts.

"An all clear from whom?" Ford finally pulled his attention away from the portico outside the car, met Marshal McGraw's eyes. The guy was young. Maybe late twenties. Dark hair. Dark eyes. Looked like he'd know his way around a fight.

"Didn't my brother fill you in? We've got a half dozen marshal and FBI agents patrolling the perimeter of the hospital. We fell short in Pine Bluff, but we're not going to do the same here."

"Fell short? That's a nice way of putting it. My wife was almost killed."

"So were two of our men, Jensen. You can believe we take what happened tonight very seriously, and we're doing everything in our power to figure out how Martino's men found Olivia."

Ford bit back further recriminations. Slinging mud wouldn't change what had happened. Besides, Ford would be dealing with the marshals for the next few weeks. There was no sense getting on McGraw's bad side. "I know. How are Marshal James and Marshal Louis doing?"

"They should recover. Sebastian said you're the reason for that. Thanks."

"I think Marshal James had things under control," Ford responded, turning his attention back to the portico.

Micah's radio sputtered and a tinny voice said something Ford didn't catch.

"That's the signal. Looks like we're ready to move," McGraw said.

Seconds later, Olivia slid into the seat beside Ford. She looked pale and drawn, the dark circles beneath her eyes giving her an air of fragility Ford had never noticed before. She offered a shaky smile as McGraw greeted her.

A woman followed Olivia into the car. Medium height with shoulder length brown hair, she shot Ford a quick smile as she settled into the car. Was she a marshal or an FBI agent? He didn't ask. There'd be plenty of time to figure that out later. Three weeks' worth of time if she stuck around until the trial.

Marshal Lawrence hurried into the front passenger seat, offering a quick wave to another man who stood outside the car. The door slammed shut, McGraw stepped on the gas, and they were moving, pulling out of the portico and around to the front of the building.

They headed east through the city and into a subdivision of cookie-cutter houses. Ford thought they'd stop there, but McGraw kept driving. Through the community, out into a rural area dotted with farmhouses. Then, as if he hadn't just come from there, he exited the freeway and reentered it, heading back to Billings.

"Is there a reason why we're turning around?" Ford asked, exhausted and irritated and not in the mood to drive in circles.

"Yeah. We're trying to make sure we're not being followed. The safe house we're bringing you to isn't going to be safe if we lead Martino's men to it," McGraw responded.

"This is how it always is, Ford. We could be

driving around for another three hours and end up two miles away from the hospital," Olivia said, yawning loudly as she finished speaking.

Concerned, Ford studied her face. She'd slept for several hours on the trip from Pine Bluff, and he hadn't expected her to still be tired. She'd always been the kind of person who could take a ten-minute nap and wake up raring to go. "Are you okay, Liv?"

"Dandy."

"You don't sound dandy. You sound exhausted."

"Like I said before, pregnancy takes a lot out of me."

"Here," he said, sliding his arm around her shoulders and tugging her closer. "Put your head on my shoulder and close your eyes for a while."

"I don't—"

"Just for a while, Liv. It'll do you good."

"He's right, Olivia. A woman in your condition needs her rest," McGraw said, and Ford wasn't sure if he should thank the guy or tell him to mind his own business.

Which proved just how tired he was.

Under normal circumstances, he didn't allow himself to be upset by people. Nor did he overreact to things. He was doing both, and seemed helpless to stop it.

"All right," Olivia said, her head coming to rest on his shoulder. "Just for a little while."

Her hair tickled his chin, her warmth seeped through his jacket, and he forgot his irritation and his fatigue. Forgot everything but how thankful he was to have Olivia in his arms again. He'd missed her. More than he'd wanted to admit. It was a miracle that he'd found her. A miracle that they'd survived the Martinos' attack.

They'd need another miracle to survive the next few weeks.

Maybe more than one.

Ford scowled, letting his fingers tangle with the silky ends of Olivia's hair. If she felt his touch, she didn't comment. Just stayed where she was, head down, eyes closed.

Ford wanted to believe she'd be safe, that God would continue to intervene. Wanted to believe. Struggled to believe. Faith wasn't the easy thing he'd imagined it to be when he'd watched Olivia head off to church Sunday after Sunday. It wasn't simply blind belief or uneducated speculations. It was a soul deep longing for something beyond self. It was a desperate need to connect with the Creator.

But it was also an understanding of just how inconsequential one human life was. In the grand scheme of the world's stories, Ford's and Olivia's wasn't such a bad one. If they died tonight, at least they'd known love and passion. They'd had careers and friends and as much happiness as anyone had a right to.

Maybe that's why Ford struggled to believe that God would care enough to step in and save them.

Did one life matter so much to a God who held every life in His hands?

A few months ago, Ford would have scoffed at the idea. Now he wondered if he'd been wrong all along. If maybe the God who'd seemed too distant to care was really much closer than Ford had imagined.

He took a deep breath, trying to still his thoughts. He'd spent his life planning and strategizing, but there was no plan for what he and Olivia were going through. No way to know what was going to come next. All Ford could do was wait and pray and trust that the God he'd once doubted, was working hard to keep Olivia and their baby safe.

EIGHT

Olivia kept her eyes closed as the car sped through the dark night. Ford's shoulder was warm and firm beneath her cheek, his hand tangled in her hair as it had done so many times during their marriage. If she let herself, she could almost pretend that they were simply taking a ride together.

Almost.

But the ride was anything but simple, and together wasn't a word she wanted to use to describe her relationship with Ford.

So why are you resting against his shoulder as if he were some kind of knighted hero?

Olivia scowled and straightened in her seat. She might be tired and scared, but that didn't mean she should be leaning on Ford.

"So, they did this every time they relocated you?" He asked, his voice rumbling above the quiet chug of the motor, his arm pressed against hers.

"Yes. It took us nearly two days to get from Billings to Pine Bluff," she responded, wishing that she dared scoot away from Ford. If she did, he would notice, and he'd know exactly why she'd done it. Because being near him still made her pulse race and her cheeks heat. It still made her want to lean in close, inhale the masculine scent of his cologne. It made her long to believe in his sweet words and gentle kisses.

And doing any of those things would be a mistake.

"Two days to get a couple of hundred miles. You must have been happy to arrive in Pine Bluff," he continued, completely unaware of her thoughts. She hoped.

"It wasn't that bad."

"This one won't be either. And I'm fairly certain the trip won't take two days. Will it, McGraw?" The agent sitting beside Olivia broke into the conversation. She'd told Olivia her name before they'd gotten into the car. What had it been? Jenna? Jessica?

"Not unless we run into trouble," McGraw said.

"Why would we?" Marshal Lawrence cut in, and Olivia was relieved to have her conversation with Ford ended.

"No reason, but the way things have gone lately, I want to be prepared for anything." McGraw glanced in the review mirror as he exited the freeway.

Did he see someone following?

If he did, would he say something?

Olivia turned in her seat, bumping into the FBI agent. "Sorry."

"Don't worry about it. I've been in tighter spaces than this and had a lot worse done to me than a bump on the arm," she responded, flashing straight white teeth and a winning smile. "Besides, if we weren't packed in like sardines we wouldn't be crowding each other. You couldn't find us a bigger ride, McGraw?"

"I was more concerned about keeping a low profile than getting a more comfortable ride," Micah said wryly.

"How much longer are you planning to drive us around in circles?" Ford asked, and Olivia chanced a glance in his direction. He was staring her way, his eyes black and unreadable in the darkness.

At some point they'd have to talk about the future. Really talk. But now wasn't the time, and she looked away, staring toward the front of the car, and praying they'd reach their destination soon.

"As long as it takes to assure ourselves that you'll be safe in the house we've got lined up," Micah responded to Ford's question, seemingly unperturbed by the subtle needling.

"You thought Olivia would be safe in Pine Bluff. You thought the two women who were murdered would be safe."

"Ford—"

"It's okay, Olivia. I'd feel the same way if it was my wife who'd nearly been killed." Micah smiled into the rearview mirror, and Olivia relaxed back into the seat. "The fact is, we're doing everything we can to make sure you're both safe. That's all we can promise."

"And if it's not enough?" Ford pressed, and McGraw shrugged.

"Then we'll have given everything and it won't have been enough."

He didn't have to say what he meant. Olivia could see it vividly in her mind—Martino's thugs firing on the safe house and everyone in it, taking out the marshals and then quickly silencing Olivia.

She shuddered, wrapping her arms tightly around her waist.

"Cold?" Ford asked, and she shook her head.

"I'm okay."

"Are you sure?"

"It's been a long night. I just want to get wherever we're going and get settled in."

"Looks like your wish is about to come true," Micah said as he turned into a quiet neighborhood of 1920s homes. The yards were well kept, the streets lined with mature trees. It reminded Olivia of the Chicago neighborhood she'd lived in and the little bungalow she'd been renting after she and Ford had separated. It hadn't been fancy or new, but it had suited her in a way their penthouse never had.

"The safe house is in a neighborhood?" Ford sounded incredulous, and Olivia almost smiled. He'd probably been expecting something that looked more like an armed fortress.

"The best place to hide someone is right in plain sight. As long as the Martino crime family doesn't get wind of where Olivia is, she's safe."

"And if they do?"

"We're prepared to do whatever it takes to make sure she makes it to the trial," said the agent sitting beside Olivia.

"And after that?"

"You'll be relocated. This time, to a place you'll be able to stay," Micah responded, as he turned into a wide cul-de-sac and pulled into the driveway of a two-story Victorian farmhouse. There were neighbors on both sides. Smaller houses that looked to be late-twenties in design. A few large trees hugged the sides and back of the house, but the expansive front yard was barren, the driveway long. At some point in its past, a garage had been added to the side of the house and the door opened as they approached.

"Looks like we're here," Ford muttered, his hand resting on Olivia's knee. His touch was as comforting as a down blanket on a frigid night, and Olivia didn't even pretend she wanted to move away. She was scared and tired, and she figured tomorrow was soon enough to reestablish the distance between them.

Micah inched the car forward and into the dark garage. No lights turned on, and Olivia shivered in the darkness, memories stealing her thoughts. Old ones of a dark figure, an explosive shot and a man dying quickly. New ones of another explosion, flames, heart-pounding fear.

Ford squeezed her knee, flashing her a smile she could see despite the dim light. "It's okay. We've made it, and we're safe."

Safe?

Safe was Christmas morning spent with family. Safe was a quiet evening alone, a good book in her hand. Safe was *not* driving into the garage of a safe house she'd be staying in for the next three weeks.

She didn't say that.

What would be the point?

For the moment, they were free of danger. That would have to be enough.

"Sorry about the darkness, but there's no sense announcing our late arrival to the neighbors," Micah said. He didn't add, "or to anyone else who might be watching," but Olivia felt the words, could almost feel invisible eyes watching as the garage door slid back down, cutting them off from the last vestiges of moonlight.

"We've got three marshals here for the night. Plus Agent Parker and Marshal Louis who will escort you into the house."

Agent Jessie Parker.

That was the woman's name.

"You're not staying?" Olivia asked, knowing it didn't matter. Whether or not Micah McGraw was at the scene the next few days and nights, things would play out the way they were meant to. Vincent Martino's henchmen would find the house, or they wouldn't, and not knowing which it would be made Olivia shiver again.

"I'm afraid not. We've got a meeting to discuss your safety later today. All members of the task force are required to attend unless they're specifically assigned to you."

"Thank you, Micah."

"There's no need for thanks. You're doing the right thing, something a lot of people would be afraid to do, and we're here to make sure you're not punished for it." He smiled, nodding toward Agent Parker. "Agent Parker will make sure you have whatever you need. She's also assigned to escort you to the doctor Monday morning."

"Doctor? I don't need—"

"For peace of mind. It's not just you and Ford we need to protect. There's a baby to think about."

At the word *baby,* Ford's hand tightened on Olivia's knee. Obviously, the mere mention of being a father was making him uncomfortable.

Olivia wanted to resent that, but she was too tired to do more than notice it. "I appreciate that."

"I'll see you in a couple of days when shifts change," Marcus said, and Agent Parker opened the car door, climbed out and stretched. There were still no lights on, but moonlight filtered in from a large window on the side wall, illuminating a space that was bare but for the Cadillac.

Olivia scooted across the seat, stepped out into cool stale air, her heart pounding in the same hard, quick tempo as it had every time she'd been relocated. Each new place had its dangers. Each move was another opportunity for Martino's men to find her.

"Special Agent McGraw has assured me this place is habitable, but we'll see what we find when we get inside," Agent Parker said, taking Olivia's arm and steering her toward a door near the back of the garage.

"At this point, I don't care what it looks like inside. I'm just happy to be out of the car," Olivia responded as the door swung open.

Light spilled into her eyes, blinding her for a second as a deep voice said, "Watch your step, ma'am."

A calloused hand grabbed hers, holding tight as she stepped over the threshold and into a well-lit kitchen. Olivia glanced over her shoulder, expecting to see Ford, but the door closed again.

"Where's Ford?" Olivia asked, taking an unconscious step back the way she'd come.

"He'll be in shortly," Agent Parker responded, her hand tightening on Olivia's arm as if the agent expected her to make a break for it.

"Marshal McGraw probably wanted to ask him a few questions." The same deep-voiced man who'd tugged Olivia across the threshold from the garage spoke again, and Olivia turned to face him.

Tall, with the broad shoulders of a body builder, he had dark pock-marked skin and a quick smile. "I'm Marshal Samson. Levi."

"Nice to meet you, Marshal—"

"Call me Levi. We'll be spending a lot of time together these next few days. Want something to eat? The team stocked up before you got here. I think we've got just about anything you might want. Eggs. Bacon."

"Bread? Luncheon meat? Because I'm half-starved," Agent Parker said, walking to the refrigerator and pulling it open.

"We've got that. Milk. Good for a growing baby," Levi continued, his gaze dropping briefly to Olivia's stomach.

She blushed, but didn't care. She was too busy going back over what she'd been told. Ford was still in the car being questioned by Micah. Why?

And why did she care?

If Micah drove away with Ford still in the car, wouldn't it be better? Olivia would continue through the Witness Protection Program alone the way she had been for the past few months; she'd have that clean break she kept pretending she wanted.

Pretending?

She *wasn't* pretending.

She frowned, walking to a small table and sitting in a chair there, refusing to ask any more questions about why Ford had still not emerged from the garage.

"Want a sandwich?" Agent Parker glanced Olivia's way, and she shook her head.

"No, thanks."

"Are you sure? You've got to nourish the baby. Even if you don't feel hungry, she might be," Levi said, taking a seat across from Olivia and watching her with warm brown eyes. "My wife just had a baby. A little girl with curly black hair just like her mother's."

"As opposed to a bald head like yours?" Parker quipped as she carried her sandwich to the table and joined them.

"Hey, it takes a lot of work to get handsome like this, Parker." Levi ran a hand over his smooth head and grinned. Both acted as if they'd known each other for years. Maybe they had.

But Olivia didn't know either, and sitting at table with them, pretending that she wasn't still in danger, pretending she didn't care that Ford *still* hadn't walked into the room, made her stomach tighten with anxiety.

Watching Agent Parker take the first bite of sandwich only made it worse. The strong scent of mustard seemed to waft across the table, and it was all Olivia could do not to gag.

She rose, smiling wanly as Levi and Agent Parker eyed her with concern. "I'm sorry, but it's been a really long day, and I'd like to get settled into my room. If that's okay."

Agent Parker frowned, setting her sandwich down on the table. "I should have thought of that. Sorry. I'm a night owl, so it's still early for me. Your room is upstairs. Come on, and I'll show you."

"Thanks. Good night, Levi," Olivia called as she followed Agent Parker from the kitchen, the tight, sick feeling in her stomach remaining.

Where was Ford?

Why hadn't he come inside yet?

She shoved the questions aside, refusing to acknowledge them as she and Agent Parker walked through a dining room and living room, stepped into a two-story foyer. A crystal chandelier illuminated a staircase and the large sitting area at the top of it.

"I'll be in a room across from yours, so if you need anything during the night, don't hesitate to give me a holler."

"I should be fine, Agent Parker."

"Jessie. And I'm sure you will be, but we're two women in a house full of men, so we've got to stick together, right?" She smiled over her shoulder as she hurried up the stairs.

Olivia followed, hesitating at the top and smiling at a man who sat in a chair in a dark corner of the sitting area. "Hello."

He nodded a greeting, but didn't seem inclined to say anything. There were two doors to the left of the sitting area and one to the right. Jessie moved to the right, shoving open the door and motioning for Olivia to come closer. "This room is yours. Looks like they've got it decked out okay."

Olivia stepped inside and glanced around, her stomach still churning. The room was just large enough to fit a queen-sized bed, a dresser and bedside table. A door led to a 1920s bathroom, the clawfoot tub, subway tile and square sink visible from where Olivia stood. "It's great."

"I was thinking it was a little rustic," Jessie responded, stepping into the bathroom and pulling open a medicine cabinet that hung above the sink. "They did manage to remember toothpaste, toothbrush and soap, so that's good. We can send someone out to grab anything else you need tomorrow. The house is safe, but stay away from the windows. Just in case."

"I will."

"Good. Like I said, holler if you need anything," she stepped out into the hall, offering a quick smile and wave before she shut the door.

Olivia dropped down onto the bed, trying to ignore the sick feeling in the pit of her stomach and the little voice in her head that kept asking why Ford hadn't been allowed to follow her into the house.

Trying.

Failing.

Was the car still in the garage? Was Ford still in it? Would he be driven off somewhere, put through a briefing that would prepare him to go into witness protection and then sent off to another state to begin a new life without Olivia?

It shouldn't have mattered, but it did.

There'd been so many times during the past fourteen months when she'd longed to see Ford, to talk to him, to be wrapped in his strong arms. For twelve of her thirty-three years, he'd been part of her life, and being separated from him had been more painful than anything she'd ever experienced. When she'd walked out of their Chicago penthouse, she'd felt as if part of her heart had been ripped out.

But staying had seemed so much more difficult than leaving.

Playing second fiddle to Ford's work, giving up her own dreams to accommodate his, in the end, losing herself for the sake of her marriage hadn't worked. She'd had to leave or she risked a slow fade into the ugly morass of resentment. Eventually, hate.

Toward herself for putting up with Ford's indifference.

Toward Ford for *being* indifferent.

She stood, knowing she needed to put Ford out of her mind. Thinking about him and their past wouldn't accomplish anything. She pulled open the dresser drawers, eyeing the clothes that someone had placed there, but Olivia didn't have the energy to change out of her T-shirt and jeans. Instead, she pulled off her jacket and returned to the bed. Settled down again, this time lying with her head on the pillow. Light still on, she closed her eyes.

The house was silent and still. No noise drifted in from outside. Alone in the room, Olivia could almost imagine that her life was her own again, that she could fall asleep and wake up to the kind of freedom she used to have. No U.S. Marshals watching her every move. No FBI agents worrying that she wouldn't make it to trial. No Martino crime family trying to make sure she didn't.

She could almost imagine it.

But the sick churning in her stomach anchored her in reality, reminding her of danger, heartache, disillusion. Reminding her that her life was completely out of her control.

"But it's not out of Yours, Lord, and I'm going to trust You to keep me safe. Because I really don't believe the marshals and the FBI can," she whispered, as the silence settled more deeply and she settled with it, closing her eyes and letting herself drift into sleep.

NINE

Ford stalked up the stairs of the two-story Victorian, his jaw clenched and his muscles tight. After an hour and a half of circular questioning, McGraw had finally finished the interrogation he'd begun after Olivia left the car, but his questions were still echoing through Ford's head.

Still irritating him.

Why had Ford been searching for Olivia? How had he found her? Had he told anyone where he was searching? What had he planned to do once he found her? Who had he called when he'd learned that Olivia was in Pine Bluff?

By the end of an hour, Ford had been ready to punch the younger man. Only thoughts of Olivia had kept him from doing so. After spending most of the past month crisscrossing Montana, hoping and praying he'd get a lead on his wife's whereabouts, Ford had no intention of ruining it all by assaulting a federal officer.

No matter how tempted he was.

He scowled as he hit the landing and a tall, plain-faced older man greeted him.

"Mr. Jensen, your room is to the left, through that open door," he said, gesturing to one of two doors to the right of the sitting area they were standing in.

Maybe he thought Ford would disappear into the room and hide away until morning, but that was as far from Ford's personality as black was from white.

"Where's Olivia?"

"Ms. Jarrod is sleeping," he said, lifting a magazine from a small table and sinking down into a chair.

"That wasn't my question."

"She's sleeping, and I have strict orders to make sure she's left alone."

"Strict orders from whom?"

"My supervisor."

"And that would be Marshal McGraw?"

"Look, Mr. Jensen, it's late. Everyone is tired. How about we discuss this in the morning?" Obviously, the older man was trying to be reasonable, and Ford should be, too. He took a deep breath, trying to free himself from nearly four months' worth of frustration and anxiety.

"Let me put this another way, Marshal—"

"Rick Case."

"Marshal Case, I've been separated from my wife for months, worried sick about her. After driving several thousand miles searching, I finally found her. Now you're trying to tell me I can't be with her. That's not working for me."

"Your wife? I thought you two weren't together anymore."

"If we weren't, then why would I be here?"

Marshal Case eyed him for a moment, then shrugged. "All I know is what I was briefed on."

"Well, your briefing was wrong, so where is my wife?"

Case frowned, but gestured to a closed door to the right of the stairs. "In there."

"Thanks." Ford bypassed the marshal, knocked softly on the closed door. When Olivia didn't answer, he hesitated, then tried the doorknob. It turned easily, and the door swung open.

Soft light illuminated the room and the bed where Olivia lay. She hadn't bothered to change clothes, hadn't even kicked off her shoes. Curled up on her side, her hair spread across the pillow, she looked pale and worn. Even in sleep she seemed troubled, faint lines creasing her brow, her lips turned down in a slight frown.

He should walk away and leave her alone. The thought flitted through Ford's mind as he approached the bed, but he ignored it. He'd traveled thousands of miles to find her, would have traveled thousands more.

He smoothed a lock of long dark hair from her cheek, letting the silky strands slip through his fingers. He'd always loved her hair.

He'd always loved her.

Too bad he'd been so bad at showing it.

He glanced around the room, looking for a chair, something to sit in while Olivia slept. No way did he plan to wake her, and no way was he going to leave her alone. He was tempted to lie down with her, but Olivia would probably rather sleep with a rattlesnake than with him. He'd have to grab some bedding from another room and sack out on the floor. First, though, he'd pull Olivia's shoes off, cover her with the quilt that lay at the end of the bed.

He'd barely touched her foot when she jerked upright, her eyes wide with terror, a soft scream sputtering to silence as she focused on him. "Ford! What are you doing here?"

"Taking your shoes off so you'll be more comfortable." He pulled the first shoe off and dropped it to the floor, then pulled off the other.

"I could have done that myself," she said, pulling her knees up to her chest, and wrapping her arms around them.

"Not while you were asleep you couldn't," he responded, sitting down on the edge of the bed and wondering how long it would take for her to send him out of the room.

"I was fine," she said, but there wasn't much energy in her words. As a matter of fact, she looked two shades too pale, her lips as colorless as her cheeks. Her eyes seemed feverishly bright, their blue as vivid and clear as a summer sky.

"Are you okay, Liv?"

"Why wouldn't I be?"

"Because you've been running for your life for months and you're tired. And because you're..." *Pregnant. Come on, Ford, get the word out.*

"Pregnant?"

"Yes."

"Pregnancy isn't an illness, Ford."

"But it does put extra strain on a woman's body."

"Don't do that, Ford."

"Do what?"

"Act like you care."

"I do care," he said, pressing his hand against her cheek.

She jerked back, scrambling off the bed and swaying as her face lost even more color.

Ford jumped up, grabbing her arm before she fell over. "You're not okay, Liv. I'll have one of the marshals call the doctor."

"A doctor will just tell me what I already know. That I'm exhausted."

"You're more than exhausted. When was the last time you ate?"

"I had lunch around one."

"No wonder you look like you're going to keel over. Sit down," he said, urging her onto the edge of the bed. "I'll get you something to eat."

"I'm not hungry, Ford."

"You have to eat."

"I'll eat in the morning. Right now, all I need is a good night's sleep."

"What about the baby? What does he need?" There, he'd mentioned the baby, and it hadn't been nearly as difficult as he'd thought it would be.

"I really wish people would stop throwing the pregnancy in my face to get me to eat." She scowled, picking at a loose thread on the bed-spread.

"I'm not throwing it in your face. I'm suggesting that it might be a good reason to keep well nourished. How about I scrounge around for some food and bring it up? If you don't want any, I'll be happy to eat it all myself," he suggested, more worried than he planned to admit.

Olivia had never been one to skip meals unless she was sick.

"Suit yourself, Ford."

"You gave in pretty quickly."

"What good will it do to argue? You'll just end up doing what you want." She sounded defeated, and Ford frowned, wishing he could read her expression. It had always been so easy before, but in the past months it seemed she'd learned to hide her emotions.

"I'm sorry for making you feel like I don't care about your opinion, Liv."

"We're having a discussion about food, Ford. Don't make it into something it's not," she said, offering a brittle smile.

"Liv—"

"Go get something to eat, Ford. It's not like I'm going anywhere while you're gone." She lay down and turned her back to Ford, dismissing him as easily as she'd dismissed their conversation.

He wouldn't walk away, though. Not the way he had so many times during their marriage. Instead, he rounded the bed, crouched in front of her so that they were face to face, eye to eye. "I'm not going to get food that you don't want. I'm not going anywhere, either, Olivia. I hope you know that."

"I said I wasn't up for a discussion about us. I meant it." She closed her eyes, her dark lashes lying against the dark crescents beneath her eyes. He ran his knuckles along her cheek, letting his hand linger there. She didn't move, didn't open her eyes, and he found himself studying her face as he hadn't in years. The gentle curve of her jaw and the fullness of her lips. The angle of her cheekbones and soft strands of her hair.

She was beautiful, but it wasn't only that that had attracted Ford. He'd been drawn in by her joy. The day they'd met he'd looked into her eyes and seen the kind of happiness he'd only ever dreamed of. He hadn't been able to resist that or Olivia.

She opened her eyes and frowned as if she'd sensed the direction of his thoughts and didn't like it. "You're staring."

"Just remembering all the reasons I fell in love with you."

"I'd snort, but it wouldn't be ladylike."

"I don't think you've ever been anything but ladylike."

"My parents trained me well. Now, if you don't mind, I'd like to get some sleep."

"I'll get a pillow and some blankets and be back in a minute."

"You're kidding, right?" She sat up quickly, her eyes flashing with deep blue fire.

"Why would I be?"

"Because this is *my* room," she said, sounding so disgusted, Ford was sure he should be insulted.

"It's not like I plan to take over the bed, Olivia. I'll sleep on the floor."

"There's no need to sleep on the floor when you've got a bed in another room."

"That doesn't mean I've got to use it. There's no way I'm going to sleep across the hall and risk waking up to find out you're gone."

"I won't be."

"You're right. You won't be, because I'll be sleeping next to your bed, and if something happens, I'll know about it."

"You're exasperating, Ford."

"I'm also your husband. That makes it completely appropriate for me to be here," he said, straightening and walking to the door. "I'll be back in a few minutes."

She scowled, but didn't argue further as Ford stepped out of the room and closed the door.

Marshal Case looked up from a magazine, his dark eyes filled with curiosity. "Everything okay?"

"Fine," Ford muttered, stepping past the marshal and walking into the room he'd been assigned. It was small and neat with a closet and a large window that overlooked the neighbor's yard. A tree branch scraped against the window, and Ford frowned, staring out into the darkness and wondering just how safe the house was.

Anxious, worried, he turned away. The queen-bed was made with plain white sheets and a thick navy comforter that was functional rather than high quality. It reminded Ford of the bedding he and Olivia had when they'd first married. They weren't able to afford anything more than the basics, but that hadn't bothered Olivia.

It *had* bothered Ford.

He'd wanted more for Olivia. For himself.

He'd gotten it, but in the end, he'd almost lost what mattered most.

Maybe he *had* lost what mattered most.

As much as he wanted to believe that Olivia still loved him and that she would be willing to give him a chance to prove that he'd changed, he wasn't sure that was the truth. Even if it was, there was no guarantee they were going to survive long enough to try again. The Martino crime family had plenty of money at their disposal. They were ruthless when it came to getting what they wanted. Ford had spent a lot of time researching the Martinos after Olivia had gone into the Witness Protection Program. With the Don of the family on his death bed, the Martinos couldn't afford to let Vincent, the only son and heir apparent, go to prison for murder.

Ford yanked the pillow off the bed; pulled the sheets and comforter off, too. For now, he'd choose to believe that the feds could keep Olivia safe, but if the Martinos found her again, that would change. He'd take Olivia and run, get his passports and

Olivia's from the safety deposit box he'd stored them in, buy tickets to France and head out of the country. He had friends in Paris who could help him hide Olivia until the trial. It wasn't a foolproof plan, but it was better than sitting around waiting to die.

Ford walked back into her room, ignoring the marshal's glare. He didn't particularly care what the guy thought.

Olivia lay exactly where he'd left her, curled up on her side and breathing the deep steady rhythm of sleep. Dark hair fell across her cheek and neck, pooling on the pale coverlet. She looked beautiful, and Ford was tempted to forget making up a pallet on the floor. If he slid onto the bed beside her, she'd never know he was there.

And why shouldn't he?

Olivia was his wife, after all.

A wife who has made it clear she doesn't plan to stay married to you.

Four months ago, Ford would have ignored the thought and done exactly what he wanted, but it wasn't four months ago. Things had changed. He'd changed. When he'd woken up in the hospital, realized that he'd been given another chance at life, Ford had known there was a reason. At first he'd thought it was simply to find Olivia and make sure she was safe, but as a month turned into two and then three, he'd realized there was more to it than that. Work had consumed his life for so long that he'd forgotten what it was like to be alone with his thoughts. He'd spent so much time rushing from one deal to the next, that he'd forgotten there was more to life than financial security. Somehow, he'd lost his humanity, turned into a walking talking real estate venture. Like his father, he'd traded a passion for people into a passion for things. His father's drug of choice had been alcohol. Ford's had been money.

He spread the blanket on the floor, threw the pillow down on top of it. Restless, but unwilling to leave Olivia, he turned off the light and lay down on the improvised bed, staring up at the ceiling. He'd spent his life working hard to be something more than what his father had been. He'd failed. Now all he could do was pray that there would be time to change things.

TEN

Olivia woke before dawn. Gritty-eyed from lack of sleep, she glanced at her watch and frowned. Six o'clock was early, even for her. She got out of bed anyway, shuffling across the room and pulling open the bathroom door. A man stood near the sink, scruffy blond hair falling below the nape of his neck, broad shoulders covered by nothing but taut muscle and smooth skin. Faded jeans hugging lean hips. A gorgeous, dangerous looking creature she had no right to be staring at.

She slammed the door, her cheeks hot.

A man was in her bathroom!

A man with blond hair.

Ford?

"Good morning." He stepped into the room, pulling a blue T-shirt over his head and tugging it down to cover a dark purple scar that snaked around his ribs.

"The Martinos hurt you more than you said," she

managed, and he shrugged, broad shoulders pulling against the fabric of his shirt.

"I didn't really say anything, because there's nothing much to say." He smoothed a hand over shower-wet hair.

"I think you're lying, Ford. And I'm so sorry you were hurt because of me." She put a hand on his arm and knew immediately it was a mistake. His skin was warm and firm beneath her palm, the contact pulling her back to a place she didn't want to be. A place where touching Ford's arm was as natural as breathing. Where heat spread like wildfire, and where love had no limits and no boundaries.

She blushed again, taking a step away.

He raised an eyebrow, but didn't comment. "I told you, what happened to me wasn't your fault."

"Then why does it feel like it is?"

"Because you want to believe that if you want something badly enough it will happen, and you've never been one to want anything but the best for the people you love."

"Who said anything about love?" she asked, flustered and uncomfortable. How had the conversation become so personal, so quickly?

"Me. And I'm also saying that what happened to me, is nothing to do with you. This," he pointed to his cheek.

"And this." He lifted his shirt and gestured to the raised scar. "They're Martino's little gift, and I want you to stop blaming yourself for them."

Blame herself?

She was too busy ogling his six-pack abs to do much more than gape. He looked good. Much better than any man who'd nearly died had the right to look.

She raised her eyes, looked into his face and her heart skipped a beat. Just as it had the day they'd met and the day they'd married.

Say something, Olivia. Don't just stand here staring at him like a ninny!

But her mind was blank, her cheeks blazing three shades of red.

"You can go ahead into the bathroom if you want. I'm done in there now," he said, a smile hovering on his lips as he tugged his shirt back into place.

"You shouldn't have been in there at all." There. She'd broken the spell of silence, but her cheeks were still blazing and she wanted to run into the bathroom and splash cold water on her face.

She wouldn't give him the satisfaction.

"Why not?"

"Because…" *I don't want to see you standing around half-dressed when I'm trying to convince myself that we're better off going our separate ways.*

"Look, if it bothers you that I was standing in the bathroom without a shirt on—"

"It doesn't," she rushed to say before he could finish.

Liar.

"Good, because we've been married for eleven years, and there's no reason for us to act like we're strangers."

"We were married for ten years and we've been separated for one." Not that she was counting the months. Or the weeks. Or the days.

"How about we save this argument for after I get something to eat. I'm starving."

"Go eat, then."

"You're touchy this morning, sunshine. Didn't you sleep well?"

"I slept fine."

"You've still got dark circles under your eyes." He touched the tender flesh beneath her eye, the caress as gentle as a butterfly's kiss.

"It's been a long few months."

"Martino's trial will be over soon, and you can go on with your life and pretend none of this ever happened."

"Is that what you want to do? Pretend it didn't happen?"

"I want to build a new life with you, Olivia. I think I've said that several times already," he responded, all his amusement gone.

"And yet you still refuse to discuss a baby that

is going to be very much a part of that new life," Olivia said, knowing she was baiting him, but unable to stop herself.

His jaw tightened, but he didn't stalk off as he would have a year ago. "I need more time to think about it."

"What is there to think about? The deed is already done. The baby already exists."

"And deserves a father who loves him whole-heartedly. A father who will be there for him as he grows."

"You said you wanted a second chance for us. If you're with me, you'll be with our baby," she argued, but Ford shook his head.

"That's not always the case, and you know it. Sometimes parents just don't love their kids. No matter how much they want to. They may be in the home, but they're not part of it."

"You're not one of those parents."

"You don't know that, Liv. I'm going to get something to eat. I'll see you in a few." He shoved the door open and walked out of the room.

Olivia didn't follow.

What good would it do?

There was nothing she could say that could change things. She'd tried telling him that he wasn't his father's son. That he was stronger, more determined, more loving than his Dad ever could have been. She'd said it so many times they'd both gotten tired of it. In the end, she'd finally had to accept what she hadn't wanted to: Ford didn't want to be a parent.

That had been okay for a while, but loneliness had set in. Ford had been gone more than he'd been home, distant more than he'd been close, and Olivia had faded into herself, lost in a world where she was married, but not.

And she'd finally told him that she needed more.

If she couldn't have children, she at least wanted a husband who loved her, who wanted to spend time with her.

It had backfired. Ford had said that he'd offered her everything he could, that if she wasn't satisfied she should leave.

"And, I did, pumpkin, but I sure didn't want to. And now I've got to think of what you need rather than what I want," she said, patting her stomach, wishing things weren't so complicated. That she could accept Ford's offer of second chances without worrying about his lack of enthusiasm for their child.

But she couldn't.

Being raised by parents who were consumed by their careers had taught Olivia everything she needed to know about what it meant to not be loved. She wouldn't allow her child to experience that.

She sighed and shook her head. Enough thoughts of the future. Right now, what she needed to be thinking about was surviving the present. If she didn't manage that, there'd be no sense worrying about the rest.

Of course, surviving meant spending three weeks confined to a house with Ford. Putting him out of her mind had been difficult enough when he'd been hundreds of miles away. Now it was going to be impossible.

She pulled clothes from the dresser, barely looking at what she chose. God had a plan for her life and for her child's. Olivia was sure of that. What she wasn't sure of was why Ford was suddenly part of it.

She'd been praying that God would give her an opportunity to tell Ford about the baby. Maybe everything that was happening was His answer.

But if it was, then why the confusion?

Olivia had been expecting Ford to turn tail and run as soon as he learned he was going to be a father.

He hadn't.

Yet.

But it was coming.

Wasn't it?

She frowned again, disgusted with herself and her inability to get Ford out of her mind. There were plenty of things she could be thinking about, plenty of worries she could dwell on.

She hurried into the bathroom, but a quick shower did little to cheer her mood. Dressed in a short jersey dress and leggings, she pulled a brush through her hair and scowled at herself in the mirror. Her skin looked pallid, her lips pale and her eyes red-rimmed. The curls she spent an hour taming every day spilled over her shoulders in ringlets that were already turning to frizz. Unfortunately, whoever had stocked the bathroom hadn't thought to include hair accessories.

She pulled her hair up into a ponytail, using the only rubber band she had, and then turning away from her reflection. There was no makeup, nothing she could do about the fatigue so clearly written on her face. And that was okay. She wasn't there to impress anyone.

Her stomach growled, reminding her that she hadn't eaten since the previous afternoon. During the first months of her pregnancy, she'd been so nauseated she'd lost weight. The obstetrician she'd seen in Billings had told her to eat small, frequent meals to try to bring her weight up. Of course, he hadn't known that Olivia was running for her life or that eating small, frequent meals wasn't always possible when people wanted you dead.

Her stomach rumbled again, and she opened the

bedroom door, nearly walking into a tall, thin man. With his dark hair swept back from a broad forehead, he looked to be closer to twenty than thirty.

Olivia stepped back, offering a smile she didn't feel. "Sorry about that. I didn't mean to nearly knock you over."

"It would take a lot more than you to do that," he responded, not bothering to smile in return. "I'm Marshal Green. I'm working the day shift. I've been told to check with you and see if there's anything you need."

There were a few things she wanted—hair accessories, makeup, a Bible, a couple of books to read—but nothing she needed desperately enough to ask the taciturn young man to bring her. "I'm fine. Thanks."

"You sure? I've got to do an errand run today, anyway, so I may as well pick you up anything you need while I'm out."

"I'm sure. I'm just going to go get something to eat and then—"

"You know you're not to leave the house, right?"

"Ever?"

"Not without an armed guard. Agent Parker is on a conference call. When she's done, she'll be happy to escort you outside."

"Great." Olivia muttered, jogging down the

stairs, and wondering what Marshal Green would do if she opened the front door and stepped outside.

Probably tackle her to the ground and call for backup.

The thought made her smile, and she was still smiling as she walked into the kitchen. One look at Ford and the smile fell away. He stood with his back to Olivia. Lean and hard, he looked thinner than he had been in December, his blond hair falling a little past his collar and making him seem like a stranger rather than the man she'd been married to for ten years.

He turned, as if he sensed her gaze, his azure eyes spearing into hers, his hard-angled face softening with a smile. "You look refreshed."

"A shower will do that to a person," she said, moving into the kitchen and pouring a cup of decaf coffee from the pot. Her hand shook, and she told herself hunger was making her tremble. The truth hovered in the back of her mind, begging acknowledgment. It wasn't hunger that was making her weak in the knees, it was Ford.

He'd always had that affect on her, but this time she wouldn't give into it.

"Want some bacon?" Ford asked, scooping crisp slices onto a plate.

"I can make some for myself."

"There's no sense in that. I've made more than enough for two. Eggs, too?"

Arguing would just prolong breakfast and the time she spent in Ford's company, so Olivia nodded. "Sure. I'll make toast."

"Already done. It's in the oven to keep warm. Want to get it?" He handed Olivia a plate filled with golden eggs and thick bacon strips. The food looked great, and Olivia's stomach churned in anticipation.

"Since when did you learn to cook?"

"Since about three months after you left me. I got tired of eating out, and I decided it was time to try my hand at the stove."

"It took you three months to decide that?" Olivia asked as she pulled a warming plate from the oven and snagged a slice of toast from it.

"I was busy."

"Aren't you always?" The accusation slipped out, and Olivia wished it back. Why bait a man who would soon be out of her life? "Sorry, I didn't mean that the way it sounded."

"Didn't you?" He scooped eggs onto another plate, piled bacon next to it and grabbed toast, then sat down at the kitchen table.

Olivia followed reluctantly, not sure sitting at the table with Ford was the best idea she'd ever had. Hadn't that been how their relationship began?

He'd nearly knocked her down and then invited her to breakfast to make up for it. They'd sat at a table in the college cafeteria, meeting each other's eyes across nicked Formica. One smile, and Olivia had been lost.

Not this time, though.

Ford could smile all he wanted, but she wouldn't agree to another go at their marriage. She'd fallen for his lines in December, allowed herself to believe there might be hope for their marriage. Look where that had gotten her—pregnant and running for her life.

"You look pensive," Ford said, somehow managing to sound as if they'd had breakfast together every day for the past year.

"I'm not comfortable with this."

"What?"

"Sitting here with you."

"We're having breakfast together."

"We're separated. Getting ready to divorce. This just isn't…right."

"We're hiding from Mafia hitmen, Olivia. Do you really think it matters whether or not we have breakfast together?"

Of course it didn't, so why did it feel so important to Olivia?

Because she cared, that's why.

And she didn't want to.

She wanted to sit down and eat breakfast just like she would if Ford were anyone else. She wanted to smile and laugh and then be able to say goodbye without her heart breaking in half while she did it.

"It doesn't," she managed to say, avoiding his eyes as she closed her eyes to pray.

"Mind if I pray with you?" he asked, taking her hand and surprising her so completely, she opened her eyes again.

"You want to pray?"

"I keep telling you I've changed, Livy. When are you going to start believing it?"

She didn't answer, just closed her eyes, his hand wrapped around hers, connecting them as Ford offered thanks for their food.

She pulled away as soon as he finished, her heart beating hard and heavy in her chest. The eggs were light and fluffy, and she scooped up a bite, trying to swallow some down, but the bitter taste of regret tainted them, and all Olivia tasted was her own heartache.

Maybe Ford *had* changed.

Maybe he really did want to make another go at their marriage.

But he didn't want their baby.

And that was something that would never change.

"Don't look so sad, Livy. This will all be over in a month. We can settle things, then. For now, let's just take it a day at a time," Ford said, covering her hand with his.

His palm was warm against her knuckles, his skin rough from years of kayaking. When they'd first married, she'd wanted to kayak with him, to embrace his hobby with the same passion with which she embraced Ford.

He hadn't wanted her there.

Had needed his space, he'd said. Needed time to think and plan.

She slid her hand out from under his, took another bite of eggs, forcing herself to chew and swallow and breathing a sigh of relief as Jessie walked into the room, smiling and cheerful despite the early hour.

"Good morning! Looks like we're having breakfast. Any left for me?" She asked as she approached the table.

"I made plenty," Ford responded, his eyes still fixed on Olivia.

Jessie must have sensed the tension in the room, she paused with a piece of toast halfway to her mouth, her gaze shooting from Olivia to Ford and back again. "Am I interrupting something?"

"No," Olivia said, Ford's "yes" nearly covering the sound of her reply.

"Well, since you can't agree, and I'm hungry, I'll take the lady's response and stick around." She grabbed a plate, tossed the toast onto it and piled it with eggs and bacon. "We'll go out for some fresh air once the sun comes up, but I'm afraid my supervisor doesn't want you out of my sight, Olivia."

"Your supervisor? You mean Jackson McGraw?"

"The one and only." She settled down onto a chair and dug into her food.

"Can I take that to mean I'm free to come and go as I please?" Ford questioned, frowning when Jessie shook her head.

"No. It just means that the marshals are in charge of you, and I'm in charge of Olivia."

"I'm in charge of myself, Agent…?"

"Parker. Call me Jessie. And we're all in charge of ourselves, but keeping the two of you safe means limiting your amount of time away from this house. We've got two witnesses already dead. We can't risk losing a third."

"Olivia isn't just a witness. You realize that, right?"

"If you're asking if we see her as a person rather than just a means to an end, the answer is yes," Jessie responded, apparently unperturbed by Ford's questions.

"I'd like to know what your plans are for

keeping her safe. How many agents are in place here? How far is backup if you need it?"

"Ford, I'm sure they've got everything under control," Olivia cut in. She'd been handling the FBI and U.S. Marshals for over three months without any help from him, and there was no way she planned to let Ford take control of things now.

"We do, but I don't mind a few questions. I'd be asking them myself if I were in your situation. We've got two marshals stationed outside the house. One inside. Then there's me. Backup is as close as a phone call, so if something does happen, we're prepared."

A phone rang and Jessie answered, cutting off further discussion.

Olivia was glad. She didn't need Ford to look out for her. She was perfectly capable of doing it herself. Perfectly capable of asking questions and getting answers, of making sure that the marshals and FBI were working hard to keep her safe.

She didn't need it, but it felt good to have someone else fighting for her.

And that was a dangerous place to be.

She'd spent too many years of her life wanting something Ford couldn't give. Too many years wanting to be more than an afterthought in their relationship. All that had gotten her was heartache. She needed to remember that, because if she didn't, she'd end up exactly where she'd been before. Married and miserable. Only this time, she'd have a baby to worry about.

Sick with the thought, she stood, emptying her plate into the trash can and hurrying from the room, praying that the trial would come quickly so that she could put the past and all its disappointments behind her.

ELEVEN

Ford followed Olivia from the room, reaching the landing just as her door slammed shut. He didn't bother to knock. There was no way she'd open it. She needed space and time to think. He respected that, but he didn't like it. When he'd woken in the hospital after being attacked by Martino's men, he'd realized two things—that he needed to get right with God and that he needed to get right with Olivia.

He hadn't bargained for a baby, but if that came with the territory, he'd have to deal with it. No matter how much he didn't want to.

Deal with it?

It's not a problem. It's a child. An innocent life that needs to be nurtured and loved.

The thoughts circled through his head as he walked into his room and looked out the window. He'd been trying for the past few hours to stop thinking about the baby Olivia carried, but it was impossible. As much as the thought of being a father terrified him, he couldn't stop picturing a dark-haired, blue-eyed little girl smiling up at him with a gummy infant grin.

And each time he pictured that little girl, his heart jumped, his stomach churned and he knew that he would do whatever it took to make sure she was safe.

Or *he*.

Maybe the baby was a boy. A little guy with his mother's strength of character. Maybe the kid would like kayaking and hiking.

And maybe Ford would disappoint the child the same way his father had disappointed him. Maybe he'd abandon his son or daughter, leaving the kid to fend for himself.

He frowned and ran a hand over his hair. He needed a haircut. He needed to check in with his real estate firm. He needed to do a lot of things, but all he wanted to do was knock on Olivia's door, walk into her room and sit with her for a while.

A while?

He'd sit with her for an eternity if she gave him the chance.

The problem was, she wouldn't.

She'd made that clear when she'd walked out fourteen months ago. He'd disappointed her one too many times, put business needs before hers to the point where she no longer believed he loved her.

Words weren't enough, she'd said. What she'd wanted was time.

Ford hadn't thought he could give it to her.

And then he'd almost died and everything had changed.

Time rather than money had become the thing on which his dreams and hopes were resting. Time to make amends to Olivia, to rebuild their relationship, to live a life that was worth more than what he had in his bank account.

He shook his head, staring out into pre-dawn. The tree he'd heard brushing against the glass the previous night, hid the yard from view. Thick-limbed and strong it had probably been there longer than the house. Ford imagined kids opening the window and climbing into the branches, reveling in their childhood in a way Ford had never been able to. That's what he wanted for his child. Not a life spent worrying about where the next meal would come from or whether or not his parents were coming home after a long night of partying.

He opened the window, leaned out to inhale fresh spring air. The tree had bloomed with fresh growth, the bright green leaves rustling in the breeze. The world still slumbered, and the quiet neighborhood seemed a place of safety.

But something seemed to lurk beneath the silence, something ugly and dangerous. Ford stilled, cocking his head to the side and listening. The morning was still and filled with an air of restless anticipation. As if something were about to happen. Something that Ford didn't think he was going to like.

He frowned, searching the side yard below the window. What little he could see was empty of life.

"Get over yourself. There's nothing out there," Ford muttered, but he leaned farther out the window anyway. He couldn't see the front or backyard, but the neighbor's yard was empty. A fence separated the two properties, and Ford wondered if it had been there before the feds decided to use the property as a safe house. It was at least six feet tall and made of what looked to be galvanized wood. It would be hard to climb, but not impossible. Had one of the Martino family's henchmen already figured that out?

He frowned again. He hadn't survived in the business world by ignoring his intuition, and his intuition was shouting that something was wrong.

He moved away from the window and stepped back into the sitting area. Marshal Green glanced his way and offered a quick nod. "Everything okay?"

"Just wondering who's guarding the house."

"Agent Parker and I are inside. We've got two men outside and one patrolling the street."

"And that's enough manpower?"

"Should be plenty. Why do you ask?"

"Just a feeling."

"What kind of feeling?"

"That it's too quiet outside."

"It's natural to be jumpy in situations like this, Mr. Jensen, but we've got plenty of manpower and plenty of protection for you and Ms. Jarrod."

"How about you just call outside and make sure?"

"How about you not tell me how to do my job?" The marshal asked with a smile that was anything but pleasant.

"Look, I'm not trying to cause problems, but the Martinos already found Olivia once. There's no reason to think they won't find her again."

"Sure there is. This time, we've got a specialized task force guarding her whereabouts."

"I'd still feel better if you'd checked with the people outside," he said, gritting his teeth in frustration.

"Tell you what. I'll go downstairs and check in with Agent Parker. We'll have our men do a perimeter check, but I can assure you that everything is exactly how it should be."

"Thanks. I appreciate it."

"No problem. I was getting bored sitting here anyway," the marshal said, standing and stretching before disappearing down the steps.

Maybe Ford should wait for his report, but he'd never been good at waiting while other people acted. Especially not when something important was at stake. He knocked on Olivia's door.

"Liv?"

"Go away, Ford. I'm not in the mood for chatting."

"I don't want to chat."

"Then what do you want?" she asked, pulling open the door. Her eyes were shadowed, her skin almost translucent with fatigue.

Ford wanted to pull her into his arms and tell her everything would be okay.

Of course, if he did that, she'd shove him away and slam the door in his face, so he cut to the chase. "I was thinking maybe you should move your stuff to my room."

"What? Why?"

"I've got a feeling something isn't quite right around here. It's too quiet."

"It's not quite dawn. Of course it's quiet."

"It's a different kind of quiet than that, Olivia. Look, there's a tree outside the window of my room. If we've got to get out quickly, it may be a means of escape."

"A tree? I've never climbed a tree in my li—"

Somewhere below, glass shattered, cutting off Olivia's words. She froze, her eyes wide with fear, and Ford grabbed her hand, dragging her into his room and slamming the door.

"What was that?" Olivia cried, clutching his hand.

"I don't know, but I don't think it was anything good." He locked the door, pressed his ear to the wood and waited.

"Do you hear anything?"

"No." And that worried him. Shouldn't a marshal or Agent Parker be checking in to let them know that everything was okay?

"Maybe someone dropped a glass."

"It sounded like a lot more was shattering than a glass," he responded. It had sounded like a window, but the only thing Ford could think of that would shatter double pane glass was a bullet. He hadn't heard one fired.

Then again, men like the ones after Olivia might use silencers.

The thought filled him with cold dread, and he tugged Olivia toward the window. "We need to get out of here."

"Maybe we should go see what happened. Or wait here until someone comes to let us know what's going on."

"You mean wait here to die."

"No, I mean that I can't believe we've been found again. Micah said—"

"What he said was that they'd do everything they could to keep us safe. That if the assassins got to us it would be because the marshals had given everything to keep it from happening and failed."

Olivia's face went pale at his words, and she glanced at the door, her eyes wide with fear. "Do you really think that's what's happening?"

"I don't know, but I don't think we should wait around to find out. Once we—"

He never finished.

Something slammed into the door with enough force to shake it in its hinges.

"Move!" Ford hissed. "Out into the tree. Don't go down. Go across to the yard next door. We'll go down there."

She didn't argue, just slipped out the window, scrambling into the sheltering branches of the tree. Ford followed, balancing on a thick limb, watching as Olivia moved from branch to branch. Graceful. Strong. Confident despite the terror she must be feeling.

Behind him, something slammed into the bedroom door again. It wouldn't take long for the door to be forced from its hinges; for their assassin to rush in. *Assassins.* There had to be more than one if they'd taken down the marshals and agent stationed inside.

Please God, help me get Olivia out of this safely. Please, keep her alive. Keep the baby alive.

The prayer echoed in his mind as he maneuvered across thick branches. He wanted to believe that God heard. That He would step in and offer help, but faith wasn't easy for Ford. He was used to planning and doing. Not waiting and hoping. Until Olivia had walked out of their Chicago penthouse, he'd seen no need to be anything different.

Then she'd left, and everything had changed.

The empty penthouse seemed to mock his busy schedule and careful plans. Each time he walked into it, he was reminded of what he'd lost and why he'd lost it.

Maybe that's why he'd gone to church. To find out what it was that had drawn Olivia there. To see if the faith that she'd spoken of with such confidence was something he could as easily attain.

But faith wasn't the same as belief. It meant giving up and letting go. It meant trusting in the invisible to deal with the visible. It meant releasing control, and that was something Ford had never been good at.

But he'd get good at it if it meant Olivia would live.

A few feet in front, she began her descent, her

feet searching for purchase as she slowly moved toward the ground. Behind him the sound of pounding continued, the sharp crack of wood telling Ford that he and Olivia were running out of time.

He scrambled after her, wood scraping his hands, heart pounding, the prayer still chanting through his mind, faith an elusive dream he wasn't sure he could reach, but that he knew he had no choice but to keep trying for.

TWELVE

The first bullet hit the dirt inches from Olivia's feet. She screamed, falling backward as Ford dropped to the ground beside her.

"Run!" he yelled, grabbing her hand and pulling her with him as he zigzagged across the lush green grass of the neighboring yard.

Something snagged Olivia's shoulder, and she stumbled, going down onto her knees and jumping up again, Ford's hand still hard around hers.

Would they die together?

Ford, the baby and Olivia?

She refused to let that happen. The thought spurred her on, giving wings to her feet.

Ford yanked her sideways and around the corner of the neighboring house as a bullet whizzed past her ear.

She tried to scream, but the sound stuck in her throat, frozen there by terror and her gasping breath.

It was her worst nightmare come to life. Terror behind. A fence in front. Fear lodged in the hollow of her throat.

"Into the neighbor's yard. Quick." Ford lifted her by the waist, and she grabbed the top of the fence, tugging herself over. Not thinking about anything but escape.

Ford followed quickly, grabbing her hand again, yanking her through the next yard and the next. Then cutting through the backyard of the third. Past a large Victorian.

Was anyone following?

Olivia didn't dare look, afraid of what she'd see. Afraid of freezing in her tracks if someone was behind them.

Beyond the Victorian, dozens of pine trees stretched up to the vivid blue sky, and Ford led Olivia there. The copse of trees butted against a steep incline and they charged up it, Olivia's lungs and legs burning with the effort, her body shaking with fear and fatigue. Gasping, gagging, she pulled her hand from Ford's, stopping when he would have continued.

The world spun, and she bent forward, resting her hands on her thighs as she tried to catch her breath.

They were going to die because of her. They were going to be shot under the wide expanse of the Montana sky and they were going to die.

"Are you okay?" Ford asked, his voice tight with worry.

"Fine," she managed to gasp, straightening, starting forward again.

"You're hurt." Ford pulled her to a stop again.

"No. I'm out of shape and pregnant."

"You're hurt," Ford repeated, pulling the fabric of her dress away from her shoulder. "Look. Blood."

He was right. The fabric of her dress was ripped, revealing pale skin and a long furrow that seeped blood in sluggish rivulets. "It's nothing. Come on. We've got to get out of here before they find us."

"We lost them back at the house. They didn't have enough manpower to station someone outside, or they simply didn't bother. Either way, we win." But Ford didn't sound like they'd won. He sounded anxious, worried and as ready to bolt as Olivia was.

"Just because we can't see them doesn't mean they're not back there."

"We'd better pray they're not, because I'm taking you back down that hill, I'm knocking on the first door I see, and I'm getting an ambulance to take you to the hospital." He tried to tug her back the way they'd come, but Olivia had no intention of leaving the relative safety of the woods. Not yet anyway.

"You're not thinking straight, Ford. If we go to the hospital, they'll find us there. And *kill* us."

"We don't have a choice."

"Sure we do. It's not like I'm bleeding to death. I've got a scratch, and it doesn't even hurt." Or it didn't. Now that they'd stopped running, the wound had begun to burn, but she wasn't going to tell Ford that.

"It's not just you we have to think about. What about the baby? What if this affects him?"

"If you're using that angle to guilt me into doing what you want, forget it. A wound in the arm isn't going to hurt the baby."

"Is that really what you think I was doing?" He asked, frowning, his eyes flashing with anger.

"I have no idea. You're good at manipulating people to get what you want. And we both know that the last thing you'd be concerned about is my baby." She sounded bitter, knew it and was unable to stop the words. They flowed out of all the disappointment and heartache of her marriage. Came from all the sadness that brought.

But they were still wrong, and Olivia wanted to take them back.

She opened her mouth to apologize, but Ford held up his hand. Shook his head. "Liv, this isn't the time to discuss how you feel or how I feel. It isn't the time to discuss anything but how we're going to get out of town without being caught. Once we put more distance between ourselves and danger, I'll be happy to discuss how I feel about *our* baby with you."

She didn't miss the subtle emphasis, but didn't comment on it. Ford was right. They had to escape Billings. If they didn't, there was no sense in discussing anything.

"There's a bus station near the diner where I worked while I was in Billings. Maybe we could catch a bus out of town."

"First we've got to get to the diner, and if I'm right about where we are, I think that's across town."

"If you've got your cell phone, I could call the diner. Someone there will be willing to help."

"That would be fine if the U.S. Marshals didn't know you'd worked there, but they do. Once they realize we escaped the safe house, it will be the first place they'll look. I don't know about you, but I'm done trusting them to keep you safe."

"I feel the same," she admitted, wondering if they'd spend the rest of the day and night wandering through the sparsely treed hills that edged Billings, trying to come up with a plan of escape.

"I think we should walk to a store, use a pay phone in case the FBI has got my cell phone tapped. There's got to be a car rental company in the area. We'll have a taxi take us to it."

"If you rent a car in your name—"

"Eventually, someone will find out I've rented the car, but we'll be long gone by then."

"But—"

"I know there are a million holes in the plan, Liv, but it's all we've got. We can't wait here for the next three weeks. We can't go to the diner, and if we get to the bus station, there's no guarantee someone won't be waiting for us there."

"I know. I just…"

"What?" He asked, studying her face, his gaze sincere and focused and so much more intent than it had ever been when they were married. It was as if he were seeing her, really seeing her, for the first time in years, and that filled Olivia with a hope that she didn't want to acknowledge.

"I'm scared."

"Don't be. God has kept you safe this far. He isn't going to abandon you now."

The words surprised Olivia.

Ford had never been one to discuss religion. Though he'd often said he believed in God, he'd never discussed that belief with Olivia. In the end, that had been one of the things that had driven Olivia from their marriage. If they'd shared the same faith, shared the same values, she might have been able to hold on to her dreams of happily ever after. But they hadn't, and the chasm between them had seemed much too wide to ever cross.

She didn't say any of that to Ford, just nodded. "I know you're right, but I've been running for months. And I'm tired. I just want to get through the trial and start my new life."

"You will, Livy. *We* will." He pulled her into a brief hug, then stepped back and looked around the wooded area where they stood. The Victorian house they'd passed was just visible below them. To their left, another hill rose toward what looked like a busy community. "How about we head up the hill? See what's there. Maybe we'll get lucky and walk right out into a shopping mall."

"If we do, luck won't have anything to do with it," Olivia said, falling into step beside Ford as he headed away from the Victorian and the safe house they'd fled.

The safe house where Jessie was.

Where Levi was.

And at least two other marshals.

The reality filled her with dread.

"They're all back there. And they can't be okay. If they were, they'd have been right behind us, urging us out the window," she mumbled out loud, and Ford squeezed her hand.

"I've been thinking the same, but we can still hope. We can still pray. There's a possibility they survived, Livy."

A possibility.

But not a big one.

The thought of cheerful Jessie lying dead in a pool of her own blood, of new father Levi, lying beside her, made Olivia sick with sorrow.

Please, God, don't let them be dead.

She wanted to cry, but didn't dare. There was too much at stake. She couldn't spare the time and energy needed to mourn the lives that had been lost.

Later, when they were safe, she could cry.

For now, all Olivia could do was pray for strength and peace for the families of those who had died.

"Everything will be okay, Olivia. You've got to keep believing that," Ford said, gently squeezing her hand again. He hadn't shaved that morning, and Olivia could see the shadow of a beard on his jaw. A shade darker than his hair, it gave him a scruffy look that added to the dangerous edge Olivia had noticed in Pine Bluff and again at the safe house. If she didn't know better, she'd think he wasn't the same man she'd left in Chicago, wasn't still the high-powered real estate broker with a passion for nothing more than making his next deal.

"What happened to you, Ford?"

"What do you mean?"

"You've been telling me you've changed. I'm

starting to think you have. You're nothing like the man I walked out on fourteen months ago."

"I hope that's a compliment."

"It's an observation," she said quickly, not wanting Ford to get the wrong idea.

Which would be what? That you're still attracted to him? That the changes you've seen only make you want to see more?

"I see."

"You see what?"

"That you don't want to admit what you feel for me."

"The only thing I'm feeling right now is sorrow, anxiety and fear."

"I don't think that's the truth, Liv."

"Maybe it isn't. Maybe I do still feel something for you. But how can I know, Ford? There's so much going on, that I can't even think straight. I just want to get out of these woods. I want to get out of this town. I want to find a safe place where I can think about what I need to do next," she said, her eyes filling with tears she absolutely could not shed. Tears for lost lives, lost dreams. Tears for what could be but might not ever happen.

"You're crying," Ford said, running a finger along her cheek and catching a tear she hadn't realized she'd let escape.

"No, I'm not," she lied, tamping down on the sorrow that threatened to take hold.

"Okay, you're not," he sighed, apparently as unwilling as Olivia to continue the discussion. "Looks like we're coming up on a road."

He was right. Olivia could see several buildings through the trees and could hear the quiet rumble of car engines. "It sounds like a main thoroughfare."

"Let's hope it is. The busier the street, the more likely we are to find a place where we can make a phone call. Hopefully, Vincent Martino's men aren't hanging around."

"Do you think they will be?"

"It depends on how much they want the money."

"What money?" Olivia asked, knowing she wasn't going to like the answer.

"Special Agent McGraw told me there was a price on your head," he said so calmly that Olivia wasn't sure she'd heard him right.

"A price on my head?"

"There's information that the Martino family has upped the amount. They're probably hoping to avoid the hassle of having to try to get to you during the trial."

"That's a pleasant thought."

"Isn't it? So, here's the plan. You stay here while I go find us a ride out of town."

"There is absolutely no way in the world, I'm standing here in the woods while you go off by yourself."

"Hear me out, Livy."

"I don't need to. I stayed in the church in Pine Bluff because it was a small town and I'd be noticed much too easily. Billings is different. There are plenty of people around, and I should be able to fade into the crowd without too much trouble."

"You'd never fade into a crowd, Livy. You're much too beautiful for that." Ford's eyes burned into hers as he spoke, and Olivia's cheeks heated.

"I don't need compliments. I need for us to stick together."

"And you think I don't want the same? The problem is, we're more of a liability together than we are apart."

"And we're weaker apart than we are together. Come on, Ford, you know the old adage—there's safety in numbers."

"There should be, but I don't think that's going to be the case for us," Ford muttered, but Olivia could see that he was giving in.

It was another surprise, and Olivia filed it away. She'd take it out another time, examine it, try to figure out what it meant. Right now, though, she needed to focus on staying one step ahead of the Martino family. The Marshals. The FBI.

That was a whole lot of people she was running from.

A whole lot of people who could be standing on the other side of the woods, waiting for Olivia and Ford to come out.

She hoped they weren't.

She prayed they weren't.

But, one way or another, she was walking out of the woods with Ford.

"Let's do something about your shoulder before we go any farther," Ford said, his words pulling Olivia from her thoughts.

"I don't have anything to wrap it with, but the bleeding has nearly stopped. I'll just cover it." She tried to pull the fabric closed over the wound, but no amount of tugging was going to hide the blood that stained her dress.

"I should have worn a jacket. Then we'd have something to cover that with," Ford said as he bent to get a better look, his hair brushing Olivia's face, the silky softness of it reminding her of the early days of their relationship, when touching Ford's hair had been a novelty she'd thought she'd never get tired of.

She hadn't, but the joy she'd taken in that simple freedom had died a little more with each new hurt and disappointment.

She took a step back, turning away so that Ford

couldn't see the sadness she knew was in her eyes. For almost four months, she'd been telling herself that she was better off without him. That a clean break was exactly what they both needed. She'd almost believed it. And then he'd walked back into her life, and all the feelings, all the longings were still there, simmering beneath the surface, threatening to consume Olivia again.

She wouldn't let them.

It wasn't just about her anymore. She had a baby to think of. A child who deserved more than a father who was gone more than he was there.

"I'll be fine for now. The cut is covered enough that most people won't notice. Let's go. The sooner we get out of Billings, the happier I'll feel," she said, hoping Ford couldn't hear the regret in her voice.

There was so much more she'd wanted from their marriage. So much more she'd hoped for.

But hope was cold comfort, and she refused to believe in those dreams anymore.

Ford didn't protest as she began walking. Just fell into step beside her. Silent, his long stride shortened to match hers.

And despite what she'd told herself, despite what she'd tried so desperately to believe, Olivia wanted him there, because being together really was better than being alone.

THIRTEEN

Ford didn't know what he'd been expecting, but finding an all-night convenience store and walking into it without being shot wasn't it.

He held Olivia's elbow as they made their way through the small store. If the cashier noticed anything odd, he didn't let on. Just greeted them and continued reading the newspaper he was holding.

"What now?" Olivia whispered, her voice trembling.

Ford wished he knew. There was no pay phone outside the store, and he didn't dare use his cell. "We find a phone."

As if on cue, his cell phone rang, and Ford glanced at the caller ID, frowning when he saw the name. Special Agent McGraw had some explaining to do, but now didn't seem to be the time to ask him to do it.

"Who is it?"

"McGraw."

"Micah?"

"Jackson."

"You should probably answer."

"I want to find a phone first," he said, walking to the cashier and smiling at the man there. "Do you know where I can find a pay phone?"

"You got a cell phone. Why not use it?"

"The battery is almost dead," Ford lied smoothly, not much liking the necessity, but unable to offer the truth.

"Got a phone in my office if the call is local. Otherwise, you can check the gas station across the road. Seems they might still have one."

"Thanks, I appreciate it. I'm hoping to call a car rental company. Do you know if there are any around?"

"Got a phone book in my office, too. Let's go have a look. You two from around these parts?" he asked as he walked to the back of the store. Sixty-ish with snow-white hair and thick-rimmed glasses, he moved with a slow, limping stride that made Ford want to tell him just exactly where they were from—a safe house that might very well be filled with bodies.

Of course that would mean he'd probably lose his chance to use the phone, so Ford kept silent and prayed the guy would move a little faster without prodding.

"We're from out of town," Olivia said, answering the man's question and shooting Ford a look that said "don't mess this up for us."

"Thought so. You two've got east coast accents."

"Do we?" Ford responded, his palms sweaty with the need to shove the poor old guy out of the way and rush into the office to find the phone himself. For all he knew, the FBI had a tracking system working on finding his phone signal.

"Sure 'nough. Come on in here. Don't usually let customers in my office, but you seem like nice enough people."

"Thanks."

"Here's the phone. Now, let me see if I can find that book," he said, shuffling through a stack of papers on his desk. Then opening a file cabinet. "Not in here."

"I could just call information," Ford offered, shooting a look in Olivia's direction. She looked as anxious as he felt. How could the guy not sense that?

"No need for that. The phone book is here. Just gotta find it." He opened a small closet, frowned into the dark interior. "There we go. Right on the top shelf. Grandkid must have put it there. Want to see if you can grab it for me?"

Ford hurried forward, snagged the book and carried it to the desk, offering a quick thanks as he thumbed through he pages. There were several car rental companies, and he called the first one, quickly explained what he'd need, the same feeling he'd had at the safe house clawing up his spine. Something wasn't right.

He and Olivia needed to leave.

Now rather than later.

But they needed a vehicle to do it. He pulled his wallet out, rattled off his credit card number and then offered a hundred bucks extra if the car could be delivered quickly.

He hung up, feeling the weight of the older man's stare as he replaced the phone book.

"Sounds like you're in a hurry to leave town. Something going on that I should know about?"

"I've got an appointment in our hometown later today," Olivia said, cutting off any answer Ford might have offered.

"Appointment?"

"With my doctor." She smoothed the material of her dress over her softly rounded abdomen, and Ford did a double-take.

How was it he hadn't noticed the evidence of her pregnancy before?

Now that he did, he could barely take his eyes off her.

A baby.

His.

Maybe it wasn't as a bad a thing as he'd once thought.

"You expecting?" the older man asked.

"Yes, but we were…in an accident on the way back home," her cheeks heated, giving away the falsehood, but the older guy didn't seem to notice.

"Well, why didn't you say so? I've got you standing here, when you should be off your feet, resting up for the big day."

"I'm okay, I just—"

"Tell you what. Why don't I close down for a few minutes? Drive you two over to that rental company? Know right where it is. They're over at the bus terminal. Shouldn't take more than a few minutes to get there."

"We couldn't ask you to do that," Olivia said, as if they had any choice. As if social norms of politeness needed to be followed when people wanted them dead.

"You weren't askin'. I'm offering. Needed a break anyway. Lazy grandkid of mine is always late to work. You'd think he'd know by now that eight o'clock means eight o'clock. Not ten-thirty. Go ahead and call the rental place, son. Tell 'em you'll be there in ten. I'll just lock the door and we'll go out to the back lot. Got my car parked there." The older guy kept up a steady stream of words as he shuffled out of the office.

Ford wanted to race after him, lock the door himself so that they could speed things along, but didn't want to do anything to ruin things. They had an escape plan now. All they had to do was follow through on it.

His phone rang again. This time he answered, knowing who it was without even glancing at the caller ID. "Jensen, here."

"This is Special Agent McGraw. Are you okay?" The tightness in the agent's voice told Ford everything he needed to know about what had gone down at the safe house. It had been bad. Worse than Ford had wanted to believe.

"We're both okay. How about everyone else?"

"Agent Parker is in critical condition. We've got two marshals recovering from non-life-threatening injuries. One didn't make it."

"I'm sorry," he said, his gaze on Olivia.

"Me, too. It shouldn't have happened."

"How did it?"

"That's what we're trying to find out. Until then, it's best if you and Olivia return to Chicago. We've got more manpower here. We've managed to get a trace on your cell phone signal. I've got agents in route to pick you up. Stay put until they arrive."

"I think we've been down this road before, McGraw. It didn't end well."

"This time, the marshals aren't going to be involved."

Ford didn't bother arguing. No way was he going to share his plan to leave town without agent protection with McGraw. "What's your ETA?"

"Ten minutes."

Too close for comfort. "I'll let Olivia know."

"And tell her that our top priority is to get her back to Chicago safely."

"I will." After they were far from Billings and McGraw's offer of protection. He disconnected and dropped the cell phone into a trash can near the desk.

"What are you doing?" Olivia said, reaching to retrieve it. He put a hand on her arm, stopping her.

"Leave it. The FBI has been able to trace the signal, and I'm not eager to be found."

"What did McGraw say?"

"One marshal is dead. Two injured. Agent Parker is in critical condition."

"Was it Levi?"

"I don't know."

"Will Jessie be okay?"

"I don't know that, either."

"You folks ready?" the cashier asked as he stepped back into the office. If he sensed the tension in the room, he didn't show it, just smiled at Olivia and held out a bottle of water and a small package of saltine crackers. "Brought these for you. Just in case. My Ruthie, she was always feeling sick when she was pregnant. Never could go anywhere without a bottle of water and saltines."

"Thank you, Mr.—?"

"Richardson. Luke Richardson. Come on. My car's around back. Don't want to be away too long." He shuffled back out of the room, led them to a storage area at the back of the store and pushed open a door. Cool spring air rushed in, and Ford took a deep steadying breath, trying to clear his mind of everything but the goal—get to the rental company, get a car, get Olivia out of town.

It seemed so simple, but there were so many things that could go wrong.

Please, God, don't let them go wrong.

He tensed as he stepped outside in front of Olivia. The back lot was empty aside from a blue pickup truck parked close to the building. Ford surveyed the surrounding area, expecting bullets to fly, but nothing happened. Aside from the traffic roaring in front of the building, the morning seemed still and quiet. Nothing unusual. Nothing to worry about.

But he was worried.

The feeling of impending trouble wouldn't leave, and he turned to grab Olivia's hand, pulling her close and dropping his arm around her shoulder, carefully avoiding her injury as he did his best to shield her from anyone lurking nearby.

Richardson opened the pickup truck door, motioned for them to climb in. "Sorry it's nothing fancy, but this is what I've got."

"We don't need fancy, Mr. Richardson. Just a ride. And I can't tell you how much we appreciate you doing this for us," Olivia said as she slid into the car. The rip in the shoulder of her dress parted, flashing creamy flesh and bright red blood. Ford jumped into the truck behind her, maneuvering so that he blocked Richardson's view of the wound.

"No need to thank me. I'd do it for anyone." Richardson closed the door, meandered around to the other side of the truck as if he had all day. Which he probably did. It was Olivia and Ford's time that was limited if the guy didn't get a move on.

By the time he climbed into the truck, Ford was ready to yank the keys from his hands and start the engine himself. Only the thought of what that would mean for their escape plan kept him from doing so.

"Seat belts on?"

"Yes," Ford said, gritting his teeth to keep from snapping.

"Okay. Let's go, then." He pulled out of the

parking lot as slowly as he'd gotten into the truck, but managed to pick up speed once he was out on the road.

Ford shifted to look out the back window, trying to see the front lot of the convenience store. A car pulled into the lot they'd just left, pulling up close to the door. FBI? U.S. Marshals? Someone worse?

Or maybe it was simply a costumer.

"Looking for someone?" Richardson asked, and Olivia jabbed Ford in the ribs, shooting him a look that said, "watch it."

"Just looking. We probably won't be back this way for a while." That, at least, was the truth.

"Pretty place, this. Used to live down south, but gave up on the heat a few decades ago. Montana suits me."

"It is a beautiful state," Olivia said, sounding as distracted as Ford felt.

Did she sense what he did? The hint of danger that seemed to hang in the air, following them as they sped along the interstate and then exited it. Chasing them as Richardson pulled into the parking lot of the bus terminal. "I'll pull you up to the entrance. Rental company desk is somewhere inside. Think they've got their cars out back."

"We really appreciate this, Mr. Richardson," Ford said, opening the door before the truck came to a complete stop. Anxious to get out and get in the building.

"No problem. Have a safe trip home, and good luck with the little one." He smiled and waved as Ford hopped out of the truck and helped Olivia do the same.

There was no time for more goodbyes, and Ford hurried Olivia into the building, sure he felt a million eyes watching.

The car rental company was to the left of the entrance, but Ford bypassed it. They had a choice of transportation now, and he wasn't going to fall into the trap of doing what was expected. His credit card charge could easily be traced, but a cash purchase would be harder to follow.

"Where are we going?" Olivia asked, as Ford hurried her to an ATM machine, withdrew the maximum amount possible and led her to the ticket booth.

"I don't know, but wherever it is, we're not going to use a rental car to get there."

"Where to?" The woman at the booth asked, and Ford glanced at the schedule lit above her head.

"Springfield, Missouri. Two adult tickets." The bus was scheduled to leave soon, and Ford was more than ready to be on it.

"Bus is leaving in five minutes. You'd better

hurry if you're going to make it," she said, accepting his payment and handing him the tickets. "It's right out front. Bus number fifteen."

Ford headed in the direction she'd indicated, anxiety clawing at his gut. He needed to get Olivia on the bus. Needed to make sure they didn't end up waiting for another ride. He didn't question the knowledge, just went with it, jogging the last few feet to do the door, shielding Olivia as they stepped outside.

They climbed onto the bus with a minute to spare, Ford's hand on Olivia's back as they found seats near the center of the vehicle.

"I'll take the window," he said.

If someone shot into the bus, he'd be the one to take the bullet. Not Olivia.

She didn't argue, just stepped aside, let him sit and then followed. Her face was pale, her eyes shadowed with worry and fear. Dark strands of hair had escaped her ponytail and hung over her shoulder in silky waves. Ford brushed them away, letting his fingers linger for just a moment. "It's going to be okay, Livy. I promise."

She met his eyes, shook her head and smiled sadly. "Too bad it isn't that easy. Too bad you can't just make a promise, and then we'll be safe."

"It *is* that simple. I'm not going to let anything happen to you."

"And what if something happens to *you?*" she asked as the bus pulled away from the station.

"It won't."

"It might. Look what happened to Jessie Parker and the others. A man lost his life today. And he was a trained professional."

"One who wasn't expecting trouble. One who didn't imagine that someone in the agency might betray him. I'm prepared for trouble. I know it's coming."

"So do I. That's why I'm getting off the bus at the next stop. I want you to stay on it and keeping going to Missouri or Florida or France. Anywhere far away from my problems," she whispered, glancing around to see if they were being overheard.

"Your problems are my problems, Livy. I won't leave you to deal with them on your own."

"You have to, Ford, because if something happened to you, I'd never forgive myself."

"And you think I could forgive myself if something happened to *you?*" He wanted to shout the question, but kept his voice low, his frustration in check. They'd been married for ten years, and it seemed that Olivia didn't know him at all.

Or maybe she did.

Maybe that was the problem. During their marriage, he'd often put business ahead of his personal life.

Often?

Always.

Part of him had believed that eventually he'd make his fortune and have more time to devote to marriage. The other part had simply chosen to ignore the hurt he saw in Olivia's eyes every time he missed a birthday or anniversary.

"I know you care, but it doesn't make sense for both of us to be in danger. For both of us to…die," Olivia said, laying a hand on his arm, the heat of it shooting straight into his heart. It had always been that way between them. Instant attraction that hadn't waned through all the years they'd known each other. It was more than just chemistry, though. They completed each other in a way Ford had never expected.

Yet somehow he'd let her go.

"Who said anything about dying? I plan to grow old with you, Olivia."

She shrugged, but didn't argue, just let her hand fall away and turned her attention to the front of the bus. Silent. Brooding. More aloof and distant than Ford had ever seen her.

Was she planning another escape? This time from him?

Or was she simply too tired to continue the conversation?

He didn't ask. No matter what Olivia planned,

Ford would stick with her. If that meant death, so be it. No way could he walk away and leave her to Martino's thugs.

When Martino's goon had sliced deep into Ford's cheek, when the blade had danced across his ribs, it had been love for Olivia that had kept Ford going. Dying hadn't been an option. Not when Olivia was still in danger. Finding her had been his mission, keeping her safe had been his motivation.

Nothing had changed.

He would keep her safe. Until the trial. After it. Because he'd learned a lot from nearly dying. He'd learned that all the money in the world couldn't buy more time, and dying with regrets wasn't the way he wanted to go.

He reached for Olivia's hand, lifted it to his lips and pressed a gentle kiss to her knuckles, praying that God would give him the time he needed to make amends, to create the kind of life he'd never dared believe he could have. A life filled with the things that were most important—love and faith.

He just needed a chance.

And as the bus sped past deep green fields and blue-gray mountains, as he continued to hold Olivia's hand, he could almost believe he was going to get it.

FOURTEEN

Olivia knew she should pull her hand from Ford's, but she couldn't make herself do it. After months of being almost completely alone, it felt good to be close to someone. Even if that someone was Ford.

Especially if that someone was Ford.

She frowned, trying to tug away, but he tightened his grip and leaned close to whisper, "Let's play nice. Just for a little while."

"We're not playing."

"So we'll just be a happy couple taking a trip together," he said, studying Olivia's face, his gaze resting on her eyes, then her cheeks and finally her lips.

Her mouth went dry, her pulse raced. She wanted to blame it on fear and anxiety, but she knew the truth. It had nothing to do with either of those things, and everything to do with Ford. The only man she'd ever loved. The only one she *still* loved.

He brushed a lock of hair from her cheek, his fingers warm against her skin and lingering as he leaned forward, pressed as a kiss to her lips. The briefest of touches, the simplest of gestures, but it tore a hole in the wall Olivia had built around her heart, left her open and wounded and not sure how it had happened.

She loved Ford, but she didn't want to, because no matter what he said, she didn't believe she'd ever be first in his life, and no matter how much she wanted to believe differently, she knew their child would never be more than an inconvenience.

She pulled back, pressing a shaking hand to her lips. "You shouldn't have done that, Ford."

"Why not?"

"Because of all the things we talked about before I walked out of the penthouse. My need for more time. Your inability to give it. The resentment we both seemed to have for one another."

"I never resented you, Livy."

"You resented the demands I made on you."

"Maybe I did, but that was only because I felt guilty for not being able to give you what you needed." He settled back into his seat, putting some distance between them, and Olivia breathed a sigh of relief, her attention drawn to the window and the landscape beyond. A few houses dotted the fields and grasslands. A farmer drove a tractor through vivid green pasture. Clothes hung from a line and fluttered in the breeze. If she could have chosen any place to live, she might have chosen one like this, where life meandered along at its own place.

"When do you think we'll get to the first rest stop?" she asked.

"Changing the subject?"

"You said yourself the time for discussing the future is after we're safe."

"We're safe enough here, but I'm not going to press for something you don't want."

"Good, because all I want is to be off this bus for a few minutes."

"That should happen soon. I just saw a sign for Cody, Wyoming. We'll probably stop there. That's where we should switch rides."

"To?"

"Whatever we can find."

"You think we were followed from the bus station, don't you?"

"I don't know, but why take chances? From the looks of things, Cody isn't too small of a town. We should be able to find another ride."

"I'd rather not."

"You think we'll be safer staying on the bus?"

"I think I *feel* safer staying on it. At least here I don't have to worry that someone might be lurking around the corner, waiting to kill me."

"These past few months haven't been easy for you."

"The past year hasn't been easy," she said without thinking, then wished the words back. The last thing she wanted was for Ford to know just how much she'd missed him.

"I know. I'm sorry."

"You don't need to be. I was the one who walked out." Because leaving had been so much easier than staying.

Missing Ford, that had been the hard part.

"Because I wasn't willing to work with you to strengthen what we had."

"I thought we agreed not to discuss this."

"We agreed not to discuss the future."

"So let's not discuss the past, either. Let's stick to what's in between—the here and now."

"Sure, except the past is part of the here and now."

"Maybe it is, but it can't be changed, so why rehash it?"

"Because I need to understand where I failed you, failed us," he said, his eyes flashing with deep blue fire, his face set in a hard line. "I don't want to repeat my mistakes."

"What mistakes? We simply wanted different things. I wanted kids and a little house in the country. And you wanted…" What had he wanted besides money? Olivia still wasn't sure she knew.

"I wanted the posh penthouse and the predictable life with a wife who was there when I needed to talk."

"I guess neither of us got what we wanted."

"But that doesn't mean we won't eventually."

Did he really believe that? Because Olivia wasn't sure she did. Having what she wanted would mean having a husband who loved her, a child who was loved by both of them. It would mean compromise and communication. It would mean believing that everything Ford said about changing was the truth, and believing that she had it within herself to forgive and move on.

They were hard things.

Things she wasn't sure would ever be, so she kept quiet and let the conversation die away.

Perhaps Ford was as tired of the rehashing the past as Olivia, he closed his eyes, shifted so that he could lean his head against the seat. His hands were lax, his profile strikingly handsome despite the scar that ran down his cheek. Maybe because of it.

Olivia wanted to touch the rough stubble on his jaw, run her finger over the edges of his scar, let her palm rest against his cheek. That's how it was when she was with Ford. Such a strong feeling of need and of desire that she was surprised she had been able to forget the depth of it during their separation.

Somehow she had, though.

And she would again.

But do you want to?

The question filled her mind as miles passed and the sun reached its zenith. The endless open sky and lush landscape gave way to houses and cars as the bus drew closer to Cody, and soon the bus driver announced the approaching rest stop.

Olivia's heart jumped, her pulse racing with adrenaline.

Soon the bus would stop, and she and Ford would either stay aboard or try to find another ride. Just the thought of leaving the bus's relative safety made her skin crawl.

"Looks like our stop is coming up," Ford said, his voice such a surprise Olivia jumped.

He smiled, placing a hand on her arm. "A little jumpy, aren't you?"

"I've got good reason to be."

"True. But you've got just as much reason to be at peace. I remember when we first got married and you'd beg me to go to church. I'd always tell you that church was for people with too much time on their hands. I've realized something since then." He paused, brushing hair from Olivia's forehead, his fingers sliding from her temple to her cheek and then her neck.

Pull away, Olivia! Her brain shouted, but her body refused to obey.

"What have you realized?" She asked, and was annoyed by the raspy, breathlessness of her voice. She was over Ford. *So* over him.

Or maybe not.

Because her fickle heart just couldn't seem to make up its mind to forget that it loved him.

"I've realized that church is for people who have plenty to do with their time. It's for people with jobs and lives, families and friends. It's for anyone who wants to understand his purpose, anyone seeking peace, anyone who wants to know his Creator. And I've realized that God cares. About the people in church. The people out of it. About me."

"You don't have to say that, Ford. You don't have to pretend to believe—"

"I've never pretended to be something I wasn't. Not for clients, not for friends and not for you. I think you know me well enough to know that."

"I do." Despite everything they'd been through, despite all the times Ford had disappointed her, Olivia knew that at least that much was true.

"I still have questions, Liv. Lots of them. I still doubt at moments, and I still think I'd like to live my life just the way I want. But I've learned that faith is about more than just believing. It's about trusting in something that can't be seen. And, right now, we have no choice but to do that. To trust that whatever happens, everything is going to be all right."

"You're right. I know you are."

"Then why are you so worried?"

"Because I want to have all the things I dreamed of when I was young. All the things I've been dreaming of for years."

"Am I part of those dreams, Liv? Or would you rather that I walk back out of your life when this is over? That we go ahead with the plans we were making to divorce?"

Would she?

Olivia wanted to say yes. She wanted to shout it, but she couldn't, because the truth was, she didn't know what she wanted. "I don't know."

"I guess that's better than yes. Looks like we're pulling into the rest area. Are we leaving, or staying?"

"You said you thought we should get a new ride."

"And you said you'd rather not, so I'm asking, what do you think is best, Olivia?"

If they stayed on the bus, Olivia would feel safe, but would she *be* safe? The Martino family's hired guns hadn't hesitated to take on armed federal officers. Would they draw the line at attacking an unarmed bus?

Olivia didn't know, but the thought of someone

forcing the bus off the road, perhaps injuring everyone on it in order to get to her, was enough to force her to her feet. "We'd better change rides. Who knows what Martino's henchmen will do if they think we're on this bus?"

"That's exactly what I've been thinking."

"Then I suppose you have a plan?"

"Sure. We get off the bus. Fortunately, we stopped in town, so we can hightail it to the nearest store and see if we can find another ride out of town."

"At some point we're going to have to contact Special Agent McGraw. He needs to know that I'm all right and that I'm still planning to testify."

"We'll do that before we leave town. *After* we've got a ride."

"We can't buy another car."

"We can do whatever we have to do to survive," Ford responded. "Come on. Let's join the crowd and get out of here."

He pressed his hand against Olivia's lower back, the touch familiar and comforting as they stepped out into the aisle. All around them, people chatted and laughed, the sounds of life filling Olivia's ears, but doing nothing to ease the knot of tension in her stomach. All the stress couldn't be good for the baby, so she took a deep breath, trying to relax.

Outside, clouds had blown in, covering the sun

and cooling the day. Olivia shivered, moving closer to Ford as he stepped off the bus behind her. She might not be sure whether or not their marriage would last, but being with him was a lot better than being by herself. Alone, she'd be frozen with indecision, not sure if she should turn left or right. Go with the crowd or leave it.

Ford seemed to have no such uncertainty.

"Let's see where the crowd is heading, and try to blend in with it for a while," he said, sliding an arm around her waist, and pulling her into his side, the gesture as warm and familiar as a friend's smile. She wanted to burrow in, forget the distance that lay between them, but there was too much there, and she stayed stiff beneath his touch.

They moved away from the bus with a group of other people, meandering onto a main thorough fare lined with shops and diners. People milled around, laughing and chatting as they enjoyed their Saturday afternoon. The simple joy in their faces, the slow, lazy pace of the day should have eased some of Olivia's fear, but it didn't.

"It's a decent sized town, at least," Ford said, steering her past a man and a woman pushing a baby in a stroller. Did they realize how fragile they're happiness was? Did they understand how a moment could change everything?

Olivia frowned, pushing aside the questions.

She'd been through something terrifying. She'd survived it. She would continue to survive. There was no other choice. "What now, Ford? We can't just keep walking until we come up with a plan."

"I was just thinking the same," he said, walking toward a small mom-and-pop store. "Let's get something to eat."

"Eat? How can you think of food when we've got federal law enforcement officers and Mafia hit men after us?"

"If I don't eat, I can't think. If I can't think, I won't be able to come up with a plan. Besides, I need more cash. It's the only way we're going to get out of Cody."

"You're planning on renting a car? Buying one? What?"

"Like I said, let's get something to eat. Then we'll figure out a plan."

"Ford, I'd rather—"

"Livy," he said, stopping and looking down into her eyes. "I've made a lot of mistakes during our marriage, and I know you've got no reason to count on me not to make more. What you *can* do is trust me. I would never do anything that would put you in danger, and I would die before I let you be hurt again."

They were big words. Dramatic words. Words that she wouldn't have expected to hear coming from Ford. She wanted to laugh them off and make light of them, but the intensity in his eyes stilled her laughter, and she could only stay silent as Ford nudged open the door to the mom-and-pop store and ushered her inside.

FIFTEEN

The interior of the store was dimly lit, the aisle stocked with everything from souvenirs to car oil. Ford used an ATM machine, his gaze focused on the large windows at the front of the building, his body humming with an awareness he couldn't ignore. Intuition. Gut instinct. Whatever it was, Ford's was alive and kicking, and it was telling him that whatever he'd hoped they'd left behind in Billings had followed them.

"Do you want a sandwich?" Olivia asked, walking over to a refrigerated display and opening it.

No. I want an AK-47 and a cartload of ammo.

Ford didn't say what he was thinking. What good would it do to worry Olivia more than she already was? If someone had followed them from Billings, they'd know soon enough.

The thought wasn't nearly as comforting as Ford would have liked it to be.

"Sure."

"Ham? Turkey?"

"Turkey," he said absently, shooting a glance in her direction. She'd loosened her hair so that it fell in soft waves over her shoulders, covering the torn fabric of her dress and the wound beneath it. She looked beautiful and fragile, the subtle roundness of her abdomen drawing Ford's attention, and making him wish for a lot more than a gun.

A time machine would do it. A way to go back fourteen months to the day Olivia had begged him to take some time off, go with her to a mountain cabin she'd rented for the two of them. The day he'd refused. Told her he had a meeting the next day that he couldn't miss. When Olivia had said she was going anyway, he'd told her to have fun, then gone over his notes for the meeting while she packed a bag. He hadn't realized just how much she'd packed until she'd walked into the office, dragging a suitcase stuffed with clothes.

He hadn't believed her when she'd said she wouldn't be returning to the penthouse. Had refused to even contemplate the idea that she might be serious about separating.

He'd been a fool to doubt her.

A fool to let her go.

If he could do it all over again, he'd have an associate fill in for him at the meeting, he'd pack a duffel and head out that door with his wife. He'd let her know then and there just how important she was to him.

But there were no time machines. No way to change the past. All he could do was make sure that what he'd set into motion fourteen months ago didn't end with Olivia's death. He looked out the window again, frowning. A hundred murderers could be standing on the other side of the glass, and Ford wouldn't know it until they pulled their guns and shot him.

He moved away from the window, following Olivia down the first aid aisle and grabbing several packages of bandages, a bottle of alcohol and a tube of antibiotic cream.

"Grab some Tylenol, too, will you?" Olivia asked, her hands filled with sandwiches and bottled water.

"Your shoulder hurting?"

"No. My back," she said, shifting from foot to foot and wincing.

A backache?

Hadn't Ford read something about backache signaling labor? In the past forty-eight hours, Olivia had been in a smoke-clogged house, had run for her life twice and had been grazed by a bullet. Was it possible that something was wrong with Olivia? With their baby? Their little girl with dark brown curls and deep blue eyes.

Suddenly the thought of losing the baby was much more terrifying than the thought of trying to parent it. He put a hand on Olivia's arm, holding her in place when she would have walked to the register.

"Maybe we should go to the hospital."

"The hospital? Why?" She asked, looking genuinely puzzled.

"Just to make sure everything is okay with the baby."

"Why wouldn't it be?"

"You've been through a lot these past few days, and now you're complaining of a backache."

"I get backaches all the time. It's from years of pushing myself as a dancer, not from pregnancy."

"You can't know that."

"Of course I can. Besides, at my last prenatal visit the doctor told me dancing and running were perfectly okay during the beginning months of pregnancy."

"It wouldn't hurt to get things checked out, Livy. Just in case."

"I've wanted this baby for ten years, Ford. Do you really think I'd refuse to go to the hospital if there was any chance at all of there being something wrong with him?"

Ten years?

Had she really wanted a child for that long?

Had Ford really been so deaf to her needs that he hadn't realized it?

Now wasn't the time to ask, or to discuss the reasons why Olivia had only brought up the idea of having children in passing, never really pushing for what she must have desperately wanted.

Ten years.

That was a long time to dream of something and go without it.

He grabbed the Tylenol, took the sandwiches and water bottles from Olivia and paid for their purchases, his mind spinning back to the years when they'd just started out. Young, brash and ready to take on the world, that's what Ford had been. Now he was older, maybe a little wiser.

And ready for a new adventure?

Maybe.

In life, as in real estate, timing was everything.

The timing had never been right to have a baby. Mostly because Ford had never considered himself father material. In the past few months, he'd realized that life was about more than business deals and money making. Maybe he was realizing something else, too. That fatherhood had a lot more to do with attitude and heart than with reliving the past.

He hooked his arm around Olivia's waist, leading her toward the restroom sign at the back of the store. A small corridor led to two bathrooms, and Ford opened the door to the first. It was a small cubicle. No window. No door to the outside.

He moved to the next door.

"What are you doing?" Olivia asked as he pushed open the second door.

"Looking for another way out of the store."

"You think we were followed from Billings, don't you?"

"I've been thinking it all along, but I'd hoped I was wrong. Now," he shrugged. "Now, I've got the same feeling I had this morning right before the world went crazy."

Like the first, the second restroom had no window. Ford frowned, glancing up and down the narrow hallway, and then pulling Olivia to a door marked Employees Only.

"We can't go in there," Olivia said, as he tried the doorknob, found it unlocked and opened the door.

"When people want you dead, it's okay to break a few rules," he responded, glancing inside and smiling at the row of tall windows across the room. They looked into an alley that appeared empty but for a Dumpster and a few errant pieces of trash. "Bingo. Now, if those windows are the kind that open, we'll be in good shape."

He stepped into the room, tugging Olivia along

with him and trying the window that was farthest from the front of the store. It slid open easily, and Ford smiled, dropping the bag that contained their purchases and shoving the screen out. Seconds later, he was standing on the other side of the window, cool spring air carrying the sounds of people moving along the sidewalk out front of the store.

"Ready?" He reached for Olivia, and she nodded, grabbing his hand and scrambling out into the alley. The scent of her shampoo mixed with the musty odor of decaying garbage, and Ford wanted to bury his head in her hair, inhale the clean fresh scent of it.

"Which way?" she asked, frowning at the Dumpster and fence that blocked the back end of the alley.

"Do you think you can make it over the fence?"

"I made it down a tree. I guess I can make it over a fence."

"That's the spirit," he said, closing the Dumpster lid and wincing at the loud clang of metal meeting metal. It was easy enough to hoist himself onto the lid and grab Olivia's hands. Seconds later, she was standing beside him. Disheveled, breathless, and more beautiful than any woman Ford had ever seen.

Please, Lord, help me keep her safe.

He prayed silently as he levered over the fence, and dropped onto the ground below. "Be careful, Liv. Just lower yourself over the side, and I'll grab—"

But she was already over, hanging on to the top of the fence and dropping into his waiting arms. He grabbed her waist, his hands sliding around her waist as he helped her down. He wanted to rest his hands there, try to feel the baby moving beneath Olivia's taut skin.

She stepped from his grasp, turning to face him, her cheeks pink. "Thanks."

"You're welcome. Let's go see what's on the other side of this alley."

"Hopefully a used car lot with some really cheap cars. Or better yet, a rental company. Maybe we could rent a moving van. I doubt anyone would be expecting that."

"Or we could hire a private plane. I'm sure there's an airport around here somewhere." It was as good a plan as any, and Ford decided to look into it. Taking to the air seemed like a safer route than trying to outrun their pursuers by car.

The alley opened onto a one-way road lined with an eclectic assortment of stores. Clothes, jewelry, food. Anything they wanted, they could find.

Except a means of escaping town without detection.

Ford glanced over his shoulder, almost expecting to see armed men coming out of the alley. No one appeared, but he wasn't reassured. Escaping through the office window might have bought them a few minutes, but he doubted it had bought them much more than that.

"I don't like this, Ford. We're too exposed out here on the street," Olivia muttered, her tone reflecting the worry Ford felt. The longer they spent on foot, the more likely it was that they'd be spotted.

If they'd been followed.

Maybe they hadn't.

Maybe Ford was overreacting.

Maybe, but he doubted it.

"There's a pay phone in that store," he said, gesturing to a pharmacy across the street. "We'll call information, see if there's a rental company nearby."

"Or an airport. Or train station. Or anything that will get us out of Cody," Olivia responded, smiling up at Ford. His pulse jumped. His grip on her hand tightened. If anything happened to her…

He wouldn't go there. Refused to even imagine it.

"I'll get you out of here, Livy. You can count on it," he said, pressing a hand to her lower back as he took a step into the street, his focus to the left in the direction of oncoming traffic. A sound to his right caught his attention. The roar of an engine. The squeal of tires. And Ford knew. He didn't look, didn't wait, just grabbed the back of Olivia's shirt, yanking her onto the sidewalk as a car sped toward them heading in the wrong direction, screaming past other cars as if the driver didn't care if he lived or died.

"He's going to jump the curb! Run!" Ford shoved Olivia forward as the driver aimed for the sidewalk, gunned the engine.

Olivia screamed, the sound of her terror echoing in Ford's head. She was a few steps ahead, and he grabbed her hand, pulling her into a store seconds before the car jumped the curb. People scattered, screaming as the driver gunned the engine again, plowed into the storefront. Glass shattered. Olivia screamed again, the sound echoed by other patrons.

Ford lifted her off her feet, nearly throwing her behind a rack of clothes as a man jumped from the car, a gun in hand. Ford expected bullets to fly, expected to die in a pile of bricks and glass in Cody, Wyoming. Instead, two armed police officers stepped into view, shouting orders, demanding that the man drop his weapon.

Ford moved, diving behind the rack of clothes, covering Olivia with his body, pressing her into brick red carpet, praying it would be enough to keep her safe.

Someone shouted. A gun exploded. Another shot followed. Bits of clothing jettisoned from the rack, coating Ford's head. He tensed, waiting for another shot but all that came was silence so thick and deep Ford thought he might choke on it.

He levered up, looking down into Olivia's face. Her eyes were closed, her skin paper-white. Fear shot through Ford. Had she been shot?

"Liv?" He laid his hand on her cheek, his heart pounding. He'd been a fool to think he could protect her more effectively than the FBI. A fool to believe they could escape the Martino family on their own. He'd read the newspaper reports, knew how many times one of a member of the Martino family had escaped prosecution because a witness had disappeared or refused to testify.

He'd known the kind of danger Olivia was in, the kind of men she was running from, but somehow he'd still believed that he knew best how to keep her safe.

And hadn't that been the problem throughout their marriage? He'd always known best, always believed that his plan was the right one.

"Everyone okay in here?" A uniformed police officer asked as he approached, his sharp eyes skimming over Ford and resting on Olivia.

"Call an ambulance."

"She been shot?" He knelt beside Ford, pressing a finger against the pulse point in Olivia's neck.

"I don't know. Liv?" He patted her cheek gently.

She stirred, opened her eyes and tried to sit up. Ford pressed her back down. "Just lay still. An ambulance is on the way."

"There's no need. I'm fine."

"You were unconscious."

"I think I hit my head on something," she said, touching the back of her head and wincing. Ford ran his hand over the spot, felt a hard knot beneath her hair.

"I should have been more careful when I pushed you out of the way."

"I'd rather have a bump on the head then a bullet in it." She smiled, her gaze darting to the officer who was speaking into his radio. "Since I'm okay, I think we should just go home, don't you?"

Obviously, she thought they were going to stick to the plan, keep out of the reach of the feds, try to stay a step ahead of the Martinos. But the plans had changed. The stakes were too high, and seeing Olivia lying pale and unresponsive was enough to convince Ford that he didn't have the tools necessary to keep her safe. "You're going to the hospital, Liv, and I'm going to contact McGraw, have him send some men to escort us to Chicago."

"But—"

"As long as McGraw agrees to twenty-four-hour armed guards—"

"Armed guards? What's going on here, folks?" The officer interrupted, his tone sharp.

"It's a long story," Ford responded, his gaze still on Olivia. She didn't look happy, but he'd rather her be upset than dead.

"How about you come down to the station with me, sir? You can explain things there."

"How about you call Special Agent Jackson McGraw with at the FBI's Chicago field office and talk to him while I accompany my wife to the hospital?"

"I'll tell you what. We'll ride to the hospital together. I'll call the fed there. If I don't get the answers I want from him, you're coming down to the station and answering them."

"That's fine." Mostly because Ford knew there'd be no trip to the station.

Sirens shrieked in the background as a second officer joined the first. They talked quietly, but Ford had no interest in what they were saying. He already knew everything he needed to—the gunman was dead, the FBI was being called. Soon, Olivia would have armed guards to protect her.

Ford could only pray that would be enough to keep her safe.

SIXTEEN

"Can I get you something to drink? Soda? Water? Juice?" A blond stewardess smiled down at Olivia, her deep brown eyes just a little too curious. Tucked away in first class with five FBI agents and Ford, Olivia should have felt safe. Instead she felt tired—tired of running, tired of being afraid, and tired of having absolutely no control over her life.

"Ma'am?" The stewardess pressed, holding up a cup filled with ice as if that might spur Olivia to answer.

"Do you have ginger ale?"

"Sure. Here you go." She poured the clear liquid into the cup, handing it to Olivia with another smile.

"Thanks." Olivia took a quick sip and placed the cup on the seat tray, wondering how long the stewardess planned to hover over her. There were six other people the woman could offer sodas to. Hopefully, she'd figure that out soon.

"Is there anything else I can get for you?"

"No. I'm fine. Thank you."

"We should be landing in an hour, so we won't be serving dinner, but if you'd like a snack—"

"I'm fine," Olivia said, cutting her off, and then feeling guilty about it. The situation she was in wasn't the stewardess's fault. "I'm sorry. I didn't mean to snap."

"It's okay. I'm sure you've had a long day," the woman smiled graciously, moving to the next seat and offering drinks to one of the FBI agents who'd accompanied Ford and Olivia.

Olivia shoved the cup of ginger ale across the seat tray, wondering why she'd even bothered asking for it. Her head pulsed with pain and her stomach was churning. The ER doctor had assured her that her head injury was minor. A sonogram of the baby had revealed a tiny well-formed infant who seemed to be doing just fine.

What would Ford have thought if he'd been in the room when the sonogram technician had pointed out the baby's heartbeat?

She frowned, not wanting to dwell on the questions or to contemplate what the answers might be. Ford had been in a conference room being questioned by the police, and that was for the best. There was too much going on, too much still hanging in the balance for either of them to be focused on more than survival.

"You okay?" Ford asked, quietly. Seated beside her, his long legs stretched out, he didn't look like he'd been running for his life for the better part of two days. Instead, he looked comfortable, confident and completely at ease.

"Just a headache. I'll be fine once I get a little sleep."

"You should have been admitted to the hospital for observation."

"The doctor didn't think so."

"The doctor looked like he was ten years old."

"He did not."

"Okay, so he looked like he was twenty. I'm still not convinced he knew what he was talking about," Ford said, offering a smile that made Olivia's heart jump.

How could it be that he could still have that effect on her after all the years they'd been married and all the disillusion their marriage had brought?

"He must have, because I'm here and I'm feeling just fine," she responded, turning away, and fiddling with the cup of ginger ale. Being with Ford shouldn't be so uncomfortable.

It *wouldn't* be so uncomfortable if she'd really put their relationship behind her.

She hadn't.

That was the problem.

It was one she'd have to deal with.

She just wasn't sure how. She'd spent plenty of time praying during the past few months. Praying for the baby's health and safety. Praying for her own safety. Praying that she'd be able put the past behind her and move forward.

So far, God had answered the first two requests. The third, Olivia was still waiting on.

"Liv," Ford said, laying his hand on her knee, his palm warm through her leggings. "I'm sorry."

"For what?" She asked, meeting his eyes, seeing what she hadn't before—fatigue and worry.

"For almost getting you killed."

"You didn't. Vincent Martino did."

"If I hadn't thought I could keep you safe—"

"We made the decision to leave Billings together, so if you've got any fault in what happened, I do, too. Besides, I'm not convinced that turning myself into the FBI is the best way to stay safe," she admitted, shooting a glance at the agents stationed around the cabin.

"I've had my doubts, too, but at least they've got weapons. Which is a lot more than I have to offer by way of protection." He raked a hand through his hair and scowled, his eyes flashing with frustration. If there was one thing Olivia knew for sure, it was that Ford didn't like to lose control of a situation. The fact that he'd been so quick to have the police contact Special Agent McGraw just proved how scared for Olivia he was.

She wasn't sure if she should be touched or worried by that.

"Did you speak to Jackson?"

"Yeah. And I gave him a piece of my mind."

"Please, tell me you didn't."

"I would, but I'd be lying. You were under FBI and marshal protection in Billings, and it wasn't enough to keep you safe. I told McGraw I wanted to know why not."

"What did he say?"

"That they're doing an internal investigation. In the meantime, he's only informed the special task force that you'd be returning to Chicago."

"Did he let Micah know?"

"I'm assuming so. I doubt he'd want the marshals wasting manpower searching for you when you're already in custody."

"Custody? You make it sound like I'm a criminal."

"The way McGraw was talking, you're as close to a prisoner as a person can get without actually being in jail."

"Nice."

"I thought so, too, but I'd rather have your civil liberties violated than see you lying dead in a pool of blood."

"That's even nicer."

"Sorry, but I can't get the image of you lying on the floor unconscious out of my mind."

"I wasn't unconscious. I was dazed."

"With your eyes closed and your skin paper-white. I was scared out of my mind, thinking you'd been shot." He scowled again, and Olivia covered his hand with hers.

"I wasn't. And now we're back where we started—under armed guard. Hopefully this time, it'll keep us safe."

"It had better."

The captain's voice broke into the cabin announcing their Chicago approach, and Olivia handed her ginger ale to the stewardess, fastened her seat belt and braced herself. She'd been in danger since she'd fled the scene of Martino's crime. Returning to the city where he'd murdered a man in cold blood didn't seem like the wisest thing to do.

Then again, she couldn't come up with any plan that seemed anything but foolish, so it was as good a one as any.

Why had she been the one to witness the crime? Why had it happened after she and Ford had conceived a child together?

Why?

It was a question she asked every day, and had only one answer to—God.

Olivia didn't know His purpose, didn't understand His ways, but she had no choice but to believe He was in control and that everything that happened would be according to His plan.

She only wished she could find more comfort in that.

"You two ready for arrival?" A short, dark-haired FBI agent asked, his deep brown gaze jumping from Olivia to Ford and back again.

"The better question would be *is your team ready?* Olivia has nearly been killed twice on FBI watch." Ford responded, and Olivia resisted the urge to sink under the seat.

"Let me assure you, Mr. Jensen, that we've got everything under control."

"That's what Special Agent McGraw has been telling me since the day my wife disappeared into witness protection. So far, she's been found twice."

"We've worked hard to keep Ms. Jarrod's arrival in Chicago from the Martino crime family and all of their associates."

"But you did let Marshal McGraw know that Olivia is on her way back to Martino's playground, right?"

"We couldn't have the marshals wasting resources on the search when we'd already found our quar…Ms. Jarrod."

"So, you'd rather endanger my wife than—"

"Enough! I'm too tired to listen to the two of you going at it like a couple of schoolboys," Olivia cut in, her head throbbing, her muscles tense with fear and frustration.

She wanted the trial over with. She wanted to sit on the witness stand, explain what she'd seen and then leave Chicago and its memories far behind. Too bad the trial wasn't scheduled for another three weeks.

"How about we concentrate on the plan for tonight rather than past failures," Ford said, his tone carefully neutral. Olivia knew him well enough to know he wanted to continue the argument, press for acquiescence of guilt and failure from the agent.

"The plan is simple. We get off the plane. You'll be delivered to a waiting car and driven to a safe location. You'll stay there until the trial."

"And there's no chance that the Martinos are going to be waiting for us at the airport?" Ford questioned.

"We're prepared for anything."

Which wasn't an answer, but Olivia decided not to mention it. The fact was, there were no guarantees in life, and as much as she wanted to believe that she and Ford would be safely delivered to whatever armed fortress the FBI had prepared, she wasn't sure things would be that easy.

Ford must have been thinking the same, because he didn't respond to the agent's words just let the other man walk away, and then patted Olivia's knee and offered her a brief smile. "Whatever happens, Livy, it'll be okay."

"I know. I just wish I knew that what was going to happen was what I wanted to have happen."

"What *do* you want? Besides making it out of this alive?"

"I haven't thought that far ahead."

"Sure you have, Liv. I wasn't married to you for ten years without figuring out that you're a planner. So, what have you been dreaming of?"

"Finding a little house with a yard and a white picket fence in a small town where I can raise a child." She'd also been dreaming of a little girl with dark blond hair and blue eyes. A little boy with his father's strong will and determination. And, if she were really honest with herself, she'd admit that she'd found herself dreaming of Ford walking through the door at the end of the day, smiling that smile that had always made her heart leap.

"That's it?"

"Yes," she lied, not wanting to admit the truth.

"Too bad, because I've been doing some dreaming, too."

"I guess you want me to ask what *you're* dreaming about."

"Why not?"

"Because I don't want to know?"

He chuckled, but there was a somber look in his eyes that only increased the anxiety Olivia was feeling. Like her, Ford didn't seem to trust that the FBI could keep them safe. Maybe, like Olivia, he wondered if he'd actually make it through the Martino trial alive.

"Thanks for the laugh, Liv, but I think you do want to know because what I'm dreaming of concerns you."

"So tell me."

"I was dreaming of that little house, too. Yard and white picket fence. A playground in the yard for the kids."

"Kids?"

"If I'm going to be a father once, I may as well be a father twice."

"You're kidding."

"Why would I be?"

"Because you don't want children."

"I *didn't* want children. Now that I'm a few months away from becoming a father, I'm changing my mind."

"And you think that means I want you in my life? In our child's life?"

"You have a choice about whether or not to have me in your life, Olivia, but you have no choice about whether or not I'm part of our child's," he said, his voice cold.

Olivia wanted to be upset by his high-handed remark, but he was right. If he wanted to be part of their child's life, she would support that. Encourage it. Because it was best for their child.

But was it best for Olivia?

She wasn't sure. Being hurt again wasn't something she'd been dreaming about.

"If you want to be part of raising our baby, I would never keep you from it."

"I want more than that, Livy. I want the family you've always described to me. The one where two people are working together to raise children who always feel loved and wanted."

"Ford—"

"Just think about it, okay?"

Think about it? How could she do anything else? The day she'd met Ford, she'd known she would marry him. She'd dreamed of one day having a family with him. Of the two of them growing old together, their children and grandchildren gathering at their place for holiday dinners and anniversaries.

It hadn't taken many years of marriage to realize that there might never be children or grandchildren and that those holiday dinners and anniversaries would be spent alone. Even that hadn't been enough to chase her away from Ford. It had been his attitude of tolerant indifference that had finally been too much. The way he'd looked at her as if she were a stranger when she spoke of wanting to spend more time together. The way he'd walked out when things got tough.

She wanted the dream he described.

Desperately wanted it.

The problem was believing that she could have it.

The pilot's voice filled the cabin again, pulling Olivia from her thoughts, reminding her that soon they'd land and that once they were on the ground anything could happen.

Outside the window Olivia could see the lights of Chicago beckoning her home. She focused on them, not wanting to see Ford's expression or to look too deeply into his eyes. If she did, she might be lost. If she allowed herself, she might just believe that everything she'd ever wanted was within her reach.

She sighed, wondering if she were holding on a little too tightly to the past. Forgiving Ford had never been difficult. What was difficult was forgetting.

The plane touched down, jostling a little as the wheels hit the tarmac. In just a few minutes, Olivia and Ford would be escorted into the airport. Out in the open, no longer cloistered inside the first class cabin, they'd be moving targets. If the Martino family had discovered that they were on the way to Chicago, there was no telling how many men they might have sent to make sure Olivia didn't make it to the trial.

As much as she wanted to guard her heart, as much as she wanted to protect her emotions, Olivia didn't want to die without telling Ford the truth. That she loved him. That she always would. She put a hand on his arm, meaning to tell him just that, but an FBI agent approached, grim-faced and unhappy.

"Once the plane docks, we're going to move. We'll be the first to exit. The most dangerous time will be when we exit the airport. Just stick close and let us worry about protecting you," he said, and Olivia figured he probably thought his words were reassuring.

They weren't, and she prayed silently as the plane coasted to a stop and docked. Continued praying as she and Ford were hustled through the loading bridge and out into the airport.

Ford wrapped his hand around hers, squeezing gently and offering a smile of encouragement. She tried to smile back, but her lips seemed frozen with dread as they approached an emergency exit guarded by two suited men.

She wanted to hold back, refuse to walk outside, but there was no denying the tide of FBI agents that flowed toward the exit, pulling her along with it.

The door opened silently, letting in cool spring air tinged with exhaust, and Olivia had no choice but to step into the darkness beyond and trust that the God who had kept her safe so far would continue to do so.

SEVENTEEN

Ford should have felt safe. He didn't. Despite the armed FBI agents accompanying them, he felt an edge of fear that nearly consumed him. Trusting that the FBI could keep Olivia from harm was about as useful as trusting himself to do it. No matter what safety measures were in place, it seemed the Martinos were able to work around them, gathering information and utilizing it over and over again.

Someone was passing information to them. It fit with what Marshal James had said the day Olivia's Pine Bluff home had exploded in flames, and it was the only explanation that made sense.

Unfortunately, that meant that Olivia would never be safe. Not until the trial was over. Maybe not even then.

The thought didn't sit well with Ford, and he tightened his grip on her hand, wishing he could race back into the airport, find a flight to another state, then another country, but even that plan seemed fraught with danger. The Martino crime family didn't leave loose ends. As long as they thought Olivia might testify against Vincent, they'd hunt her down to try and stop her.

A dark sedan idled a few feet away, and Ford could clearly see two men in the front seat. An armed guard opened the back door as they approached, his sharp gaze scanning the area. The scene seemed liked something out of a spy thriller, but it was real life. Ford's life. Olivia's. The baby's.

The thought no longer filled him with dread.

He wanted the baby as much as he wanted the life he'd described to Olivia.

Please, Lord, let us have it. Give us that second chance, he prayed as Olivia slid into the middle of the backseat. An agent was already seated on her far side, and Ford slid in next to her, his pulse racing with adrenaline.

So far, so good. No bullets flying. No cars speeding toward them. Maybe they had flown in under Martino radar.

Maybe.

And maybe the Martino family was biding its time, waiting for the perfect opportunity to strike.

Which would be when? On the road? During the trial? At whatever destination Ford and Olivia were being brought to?

Ford tried to think it through as the car pulled out onto the highway. There wasn't a whole lot of open road in Chicago, but the driver aimed for the edge of town, driving them out of the city and into suburban sprawl. The road was congested, the traffic heavy and slow moving. Would Martino dare to strike now?

He shifted in his seat, turning to look out the back window.

"We've got a car of agents following. If Martino had men waiting at the airport, there's no sign of them now," the driver said, and Ford met the man's eyes in the rearview mirror.

"I wish I were as confident of that as you are."

"Hey, I'm not saying something can't go wrong. I'm just saying that for right now we're in the clear."

"Where are we going?" Olivia asked, and Ford wondered if she actually thought she'd get an answer. So far, the FBI hadn't been very forthcoming with information.

"I'm afraid I'm not at liberty to say, ma'am. We've got a ways to go, though, so you may as well make yourself comfortable."

"And wherever we're going, we're going to stay there until the trial? Or will there be another location after this?"

"Sounds like you'll be staying there. Special

Agent McGraw said the prosecuting attorney will probably want to start preparing you for the trial in a few weeks, so we'll want you close the district office."

"A few weeks? The trial is scheduled for the end of April. That's less than three weeks away."

"It's been rescheduled for May."

"Rescheduled? By whom?" Ford broke in, wondering why they hadn't been informed of the change sooner. Three weeks in protective custody was something he could imagine. A month or more was something he didn't even want to consider.

"My guess would be the prosecuting attorney, but who knows? All I know is what I've been told. The trial is in May. Not April."

"I'd like to speak with McGraw about that."

"You're welcome to contact him as soon as we reach the safe house. As a matter of fact, I wouldn't be surprised if he was there to meet us. Seems to me, he had some things he wanted to say to you, too."

Ford had no doubt about that. He'd spoken to McGraw briefly before he was questioned by the Cody police. The special agent had made no bones about his irritation. He'd expected Olivia and Ford to follow orders and to stay put. Which proved that he didn't know much about either of them.

"I'll be happy to hear whatever it is McGraw

wants to say to me *after* he explains why the trial date has been moved."

"That's between you and Special Agent McGraw. My only concern is getting you to the safe house in one piece," the agent responded, frowning into the rearview mirror. "Looks like we've got company coming."

The agent sitting beside Olivia glanced back and Ford did the same. A dark car kept pace a few car lengths behind their vehicle, and at first Ford thought that was the company that was being referred to. Then he noticed the white work van. Dirty and neglected, it didn't look like much and wouldn't have been noticeable at all if it hadn't been moving quickly through the waning traffic. Five cars away. Then four. It pulled up beside the dark car, swerved sideways, nearly forcing the other vehicle off the road.

Seconds later, it swerved again, this time side-swiping the smaller vehicle. The car spun away, slamming into a cement divider.

Someone cursed, the sound sharp and harsh, and Olivia tensed, pivoting so that she could see the approaching van. "Dear God, help us."

Ford heard her whispered prayer above the sound of their driver shouting into his radio, above the pounding of his heart, above his own petitions to God. It echoed in his head as the driver accelerated, speeding through the remaining traffic and trying to put distance between their car and the van.

It wasn't going to work.

Ford could have told the agent that.

All the defensive driving in the world couldn't prevent what was about to happen. Despite its neglected appearance, the van seemed to pick up speed with ease, bearing down on the car without any effort.

"Give us some more gas!" The agent beside Olivia shouted, and the car pulled ahead of the van again. Not by much, and not enough. Ford braced himself, throwing his arm around Olivia's shoulders as the van rammed into the bumper of their car, propelling it forward.

Olivia screamed, her terror filling the car, mixing with the sound of mumbled curses, the harsh shouts coming from the radio.

"Hold on!" the driver shouted, braking hard as he swerved to shoulder. The van shot past, then squealed to a stop. The back door flew open, and several men spilled out onto the road, guns in hands, weapons already firing.

Glass exploded and the driver of the car slumped over the steering wheel, the long high-pitched moan of the horn filling the car. The agent beside Olivia threw open the door, ducking low, the crack of his weapon joining the horn's mournful cry.

More glass exploded, and Ford shoved Olivia down, covering her with his body as the agent in the front seat pushed his door open, joining his comrade in the gunfight.

Ford's ears rang from the sound of gunfire and from the blaring horn, and he could no longer tell where the shots were coming from. The FBI agents? Martino's hired guns?

The agent closest to Ford, flew back, landing in a heap on the ground, his gun clattering a few inches away. Ford needed that gun. It was Olivia's only chance.

He pressed his mouth close to her ear, nearly shouting to be heard about the cacophony of noise. "I've got to get a weapon or we're not going to make it out of this alive."

"What are you talking about? You're not going out there," she shouted in reply, shifting so that she could look up into his face. Her skin was chalk-white, her eyes so blue it almost hurt to look at them, and Ford knew he would do anything to keep her safe.

"I don't have a choice. Stay down," he said, gently pushing her back down. "And, whatever you do, don't move!"

If she responded, he didn't hear, he was too focused on his goal—get out of the car, get the gun, make sure that he had some way of protecting Olivia.

He slipped out of the car, ducking behind the open door and staying low as he ran to the fallen agent. He didn't have time to check for a pulse or administer first aid. Not with bullets still flying. He reached for the gun, flying backward as something slammed into his chest. High. To the right.

You're still alive, so keep moving.

The command echoed through his head, filled mind, and he obeyed, reaching for the gun again. Lifting it, pivoting hard on his knees. No time for pain. No time for losing consciousness. There was too much at stake. Olivia. The baby.

Strobe lights flashed, doors slammed.

Backup arriving?

Ford didn't know. Couldn't take the time to look. Someone was running toward him, running toward the car, aiming a gun at the open door and the seat where Olivia lay. He didn't think. Didn't worry about the ramifications of what he was going to do. Just aimed and fired, watching as the assailant fell.

Olivia.

Ford wanted to shout her name, but could get nothing past the hot, coppery taste in his mouth. He stumbled to his feet, his head swimming, the gun dropping from his hand. The gunfire had ceased, and other sounds filled the sudden stillness. Voices shouting. Car doors slamming. The incessant horn still screaming.

Ford barely heard them. His focus was on the car. On Olivia.

Was she okay?

"Livy?" He managed to rasp out as he peered into the car. To his relief, she sat up, her face streaked with tears.

He reached for her, pulling her from the car and into his arms. "It's okay, Liv. It's over."

"Don't ever do that again, Ford. Ever."

"If it means the difference between you living and dying, I'll do it again a hundred times."

"What about you living or dying? You could have been killed? If I didn't have the baby to think about, I'd have gone out and pulled you back into the car by your hair." She stepped out of his arms, and he swayed, the world spinning a little with her movement.

"You're hurt," she said, her hand pressing against his chest, her eyes swimming with more tears.

"I'll be okay."

"You're bleeding badly, Ford. Sit down. I've got to get help." She slipped an arm around his waist, urging him to the car.

He planned to tell her that he didn't need help, but his legs had other ideas and he slid into the car. It was that or collapse onto the ground.

Olivia started to move away, but he grabbed her

hand, holding her in place. "Stay here. The police will figure out that it's safe and move in soon enough. The last thing I want is for them to mistake you for a bad guy and start shooting."

"Do you really think I'm going to sit here and watch you bleed to death while we wait for the police and FBI to figure things out?"

"I'm not going to die," he said, gritting his teeth as pain shot through his chest.

"Like the FBI wasn't going to let the Martinos find us again? Sorry, I'm not going to take any chances that you're wrong." She pulled her hand from his, leaned forward and pressed a gentle kiss to his lips. "Be okay, Ford, because I really don't want to raise our baby alone."

"You don't have to worry, Livy. I'm too ornery to die," he said, but the world was spinning and blackness was edging in.

"You'd better be," she said, her lips brushing his again before she backed out of the car.

He wanted to grab her dress, force her to stay with him, but his body wouldn't cooperate. Searing pain shot through his chest again, stealing his breath, nearly stealing his consciousness. Maybe the wound was worse than he thought. Maybe he *was* going to die, but he'd accomplished his goal. Olivia was alive. The baby was. God had intervened once again, protecting the only woman Ford had ever loved. Protecting the child they'd conceived. Whether he lived or died, at least Ford had that.

But there was so much more that he wanted.

Just a chance, Lord. A chance to do things Your way instead of mine. A chance to cherish the gifts You've given me. Olivia. Our baby.

Just a chance.

The prayer was still running through his mind as more pain exploded through his chest and the darkness that had been threatening blocked his vision, shutting out his thoughts, his fears, his hopes until there was nothing but darkness and the gentle touch of lips on his forehead, the softness of fingers resting against his neck, the warmth of tears dropping onto his cheek.

Olivia?

Or just a trick of the darkness?

Ford didn't know, couldn't care as the blackness carried him farther away from the car and from his pain.

EIGHTEEN

Olivia paced the length of the small waiting room for what seemed like the hundredth time, ignoring the concerned look of the FBI agent who was standing guard by the door. She didn't care if her endless pacing was causing him concern, didn't care if it wore holes in the rug. All she cared about was Ford and the fact that he'd been in surgery for five hours and there was still no word from the doctor.

"Pacing isn't going to get your husband out of surgery any sooner, Ms. Jarrod. Why don't you sit down? Let me send someone to get you something to eat and drink?" The agent suggested, his green eyes searching Olivia's face as if he expected her to break down at any moment.

"I'm fine. Thanks for offering, though," she responded, her voice having an edge of irritation that had nothing to do with the agent's question and everything to do with fear and worry.

What was taking so long?"

The surgeon had said three or four hours. Not five or six. Was Ford okay? Had something gone wrong? Had he…

She refused to go there. Refused to even contemplate the possibility that Ford had died on the operating table.

A soft knock sounded on the door, and the agent motioned Olivia back as he pulled it open.

Olivia tensed, expecting to see the surgeon, wondering if she'd be able to know Ford's fate by simply reading the doctor's face. But instead of the gray-haired surgeon, a tall, dark-haired man walked in. Broad-shouldered and confident, he was someone Olivia hadn't seen in almost four months, but she recognized him immediately.

"Jackson." She stepped toward him, her heart sinking as she looked into his face. "What is it? Has something happened to Ford?"

"As far as I know, he's holding his own," Jackson responded, his gaze somber and filled with so much compassion Olivia's eyes filled with tears. She refused to let them fall. If she did, she wasn't sure she'd be able to stop them again.

"Then why are you looking at me like that?"

"Because I owe you an apology. Tonight shouldn't have happened. We fell short on our job of protecting you. I blame myself for that."

"Why? You're not the only one who was responsible for keeping me safe."

"But I *am* the one who looked you in the eye in
December and told you that we'd make sure the
Martino family couldn't get to you."

"You did your best. The agents that were with
us tonight, they did everything they could to
protect me. I wish…" Olivia's voice broke and she
couldn't continue.

"They knew the risk going into this, and they
knew their duty."

"Are they…" She couldn't make herself say
what she was thinking. Had the agents who'd
fought to protect her, given their lives to keep her
safe?

"Two are in the hospital. One didn't make it."

"I'm so sorry." She tried to fight back tears, but
they fell anyway, spilling down her cheeks and
onto her shirt. She was too tired to wipe them away.

"Me, too. Come on," he said, taking her arm.
"Let's sit down and chat about what happens next."

"I'm not in the frame of mind for sitting or
chatting," Olivia said, but she allowed herself to be
led to the small sofa that stood against one wall.

"I'm not, either, but it's got to be done."
McGraw dropped onto the sofa and motioned for
Olivia to do the same. He looked tired and slightly
haggard, as if the day had aged him.

"Jackson, I can't tell you how sorry I am for what your agency has lost tonight. What those agents' families have lost."

"We were fortunate to only lose one man tonight. But one man is one too many, and we are all grieving his loss."

"Please tell his family…" What? What could possibly be said that could make his death more palatable? Nothing. Olivia knew it, but continued anyway, desperate to offer them some small bit of comfort. "Tell them he was a true hero."

"I already have," Jackson said, running a hand over his hair.

"Do you know how it happened? How the Martinos knew we'd arrived in Chicago?"

"If I knew that, I'd be a lot happier. Right now, I'm leaning toward believing that they heard you'd left Billings and were staking out the airport expecting that you'd arrive back in Chicago eventually."

"So no matter when we arrived, we wouldn't have been safe," Olivia said, more to herself than to Jackson, but he nodded.

"It seems that might be the case, but we're investigating and will hopefully know more soon. For now, we've got armed guards stationed outside this room and your husband's. We've also got patrols outside the hospital. No one will get to you again."

"I've heard that before."

"This time you can believe it."

"There's a leak in the system somewhere Jackson. Until you find it—"

"You'll be safe. There is no doubt about that Only a handful of men know you're here. All of them were handpicked for the job of protecting you. I'd trust any of them with my life. But that's not what I came here to discuss. I wanted to talk to you about Martino's trial."

"I heard it had been postponed."

"Until the beginning of May. Not too far off from when we'd originally planned it."

"I guess there's a reason for that."

"We're continuing to build the case against Vincent Martino."

"Build the case against him? I watched him murder a man in cold blood!"

"And your testimony is vital to the state's case but the state's attorney general is waiting on more forensic evidence."

"I was hoping to get the trial over with sooner rather than later."

"We were all hoping for that, but the last thing we want is to go to trial and lose."

"Do you think that's possible?" The idea of Vincent Martino wandering Chicago as a free man made Olivia shudder.

"No, but he's weaseled out of too many charges for us to take anything for granted. We have a good witness. We've got forensic evidence. We just need to make sure our case is air tight. I know an extra couple of weeks under our protection isn't what you want, but I hope you'll continue to cooperate with us."

"Another couple of weeks isn't going to kill me." She hoped.

"Good. Once your husband is out of surgery, we'll escort you to his room. You'll stay there under armed protection until he's ready to leave the hospital."

"And then?"

"We'll move you to FBI headquarters where you'll stay until the trial."

"That sounds…comfortable."

"It will be," he said, offering a tired smile. "And it will be a lot safer than moving you to a safe house in the area. The Martino family didn't become as powerful as it is by being foolish. No way will they launch an attack on our district office."

"They attacked an armed vehicle."

"The men in that van weren't part of the Martino family. They were hired guns too stupid to know the kind of mistake they were making. The Martinos are smarter than that. They'll bide their time, wait until they think they have a chance of being successful. Then they'll strike."

"I don't think I like the sound of that."

"Me, neither. The good news is, they're not going to have an opportunity to strike. Security is so tight around you and Ford that no one is going to get within a mile of you without me knowing about it."

"A mile?"

"An exaggeration, but not much of one. We *will* keep you safe, Olivia. You have my word on it."

Olivia wanted to believe him, could almost hope that this time Jackson was right and that she really would be safe.

Someone knocked on the door, and Jackson stood, following the other agent to the door.

Both men stepped back as Ford's surgeon walked in. Still dressed in blood stained scrubs, his salt-and-pepper hair mussed, he looked more upbeat than tired, and Olivia's heart leaped.

Hope she hadn't even dared feel welled up as she stood and hurried across the room. "How is he?"

"Better than he's got a right to be. The bullet was lodged millimeters from a major artery."

"But he's going to be okay?"

"Barring any unforeseen complications, your husband should make a full recovery."

"Thank you, so much!" Olivia threw herself at

the unsuspecting doctor, but he didn't seem to mind the bear hug she offered.

When she finally had the good sense to release her hold and step back, he smiled. "I'm not the only one you should be thanking. There was an entire team of people in the operating room, and I'm not convinced we were the only ones there. I've seen gunshot wounds less serious than your husband's take a life. Some people would say he's lucky, I say he's blessed."

"He is," Olivia said, smiling past tears of relief. "When can I see him?"

"He's in recovery, so I'll have the nurse come get you. I'm afraid your entourage will have to wait outside the room. We only allow one visitor at a time," he said, shooting a glance at the two agents.

"No problem, but have the nurse close the window shades before Ms. Jarrod enters the room," Jackson responded, and the surgeon nodded.

"I'll let her know. The last thing we want is another gunshot wound to treat. I'll be around for a while longer just in case there's post-op bleeding, but if I don't see you before I leave, I'll check in with you in the morning, Ms. Jarrod."

"Thank you again, doctor."

And thank You, *God. Thank You.*

The prayer chanted through Olivia's mind as the

surgeon exited the room and was still there as a nurse arrived. A prayer of praise and of hope and filled with more joy than Olivia had ever felt.

Ford was alive. He'd make a full recovery.

And they would get through the trial.

They would begin a new life together.

She had to believe that. Had to hold on to it.

It only took a few minutes for Olivia's FBI guards to coordinate themselves, but it seemed like an eternity. She paced the small waiting room a few more times, anxious to see her husband. As reassured as she was by the surgeon's words, she wanted to see for herself that Ford had survived.

Finally, Jackson motioned for Olivia to step out of the waiting room. Several agents surrounded her as she was hurried down the hall and into an elevator. She couldn't see past the wall of bodies, but if she could she was sure she'd see curiosity in the eyes of everyone they passed. Pressed in on all sides, she felt like a prisoner, but being a prisoner was a whole lot better than being dead, and she didn't complain.

The nurse walking beside Olivia seemed unfazed by the procession, her sharp gaze raking over each of the agents in turn. "Gotta say, I wouldn't mind being surrounded by this group of men every day for the rest of my life."

Her comment surprised a laugh out of Olivia.

"You might if you knew that they were the only thing standing between you and death."

"Don't know about that. They're one good-looking group of men. They can be my bodyguards any day."

Olivia wasn't sure, but she thought one of the agents actually blushed. It was almost enough to take her mind off of Ford.

Almost.

"Is my husband awake, Nurse…"

"Just call me Rachel. Everyone does. And your man is awake. Awake and asking for you. He must love you something fierce because he was calling your name before he even came out of anesthesia. Me? If I had a man like that, I wouldn't be commenting on the good looks of your personal body guards. I'd be like you, wanting to ditch the crowd and have some quality alone time with my guy."

Now it was Olivia's turn to blush.

"Ford is a good man."

A man who'd saved her life.

Just the thought made Olivia's stomach churn. When he'd told her he was going for a weapon, she'd wanted desperately to jump from the car and pull him back in. Only the thoughts of the fragile life she carried had kept her from doing so.

"Now, listen, dear heart, your husband is looking a little rough around the edges," Rachel said as they approached a door at the end of the hall. Two armed police officers were seated in chairs on either side of it. Olivia wasn't sure, but she thought a man leaning against a wall a few feet away might be an undercover officer.

Jackson had been telling the truth. The FBI wasn't taking any chances, and no expense was being spared to keep Olivia and Ford safe. For the first time in a long time, she felt safe.

"If you'd rather wait to see him after he's feeling a little better, it's okay. He told me about the pregnancy, and he's worried something fierce that you're overdoing things. Tried to tell him we women were made of hardier stock than the average man, but he'd have none of it. So, I've got to ask, you ready for this? Or would you rather rest up a little before you go in?" Rachel asked, her sharp eyes suddenly soft with concern.

"I'm fine. I want to see him," Olivia hurried to assure her, anxious to step into the room, to see that Ford really was going to be okay.

"You ever seen someone hooked up to machines, tubes coming out of his chest?"

"No."

"Me? I've seen more than one person pass out after seeing a loved one hooked to machines. We don't want to be scraping you off the floor."

"I'll be okay."

"I thought you would, but I had to mention it. I've already closed the curtains. You ready to go see your husband?"

"Yes."

"Then let's get this show on the road," Rachel said, pushing the door open. Olivia took a step to follow, stopping short when an agent put a hand on her shoulder, holding her in place.

"Let one of us go in first. Just to be sure."

"There's two armed guards—"

"Procedure, Olivia," Jackson cut in. "It's just an extra measure of precaution."

And the sooner she shut up and let them do their job the quicker she'd be in the room with Ford. Olivia nodded and waited impatiently as one of the men followed the nurse into the room.

"All clear," he said as he returned, nodding at one of the two police officers. Neither looked happy to have the FBI double-checking their efforts, but they had the good grace not to say anything. Not that Olivia would have hung around to listen to the conversation.

She hurried into the dimly lit room, her pulse racing with anxiety. The hum of machines and gentle beep of a heart monitor were the only sound, and she approached the bed quietly. Ford lay still, his eyes closed. A thick blanket covered him from the shoulders down. Blond hair dull, his skin ashen, it seemed that the vitality that made Ford who he was had drained out of him, and for a moment Olivia thought she was looking at someone else's husband.

Her hand shook as she brushed a lock of hair from his forehead and then placed her palm against the cool flesh of cheek.

"Ford," she whispered, her voice catching, her stomach twisting with sorrow. He'd nearly died to keep her safe, and all the things she'd once thought so important—missed birthdays and dinners, weekend getaways spent alone, forgotten anniversaries, conversations cut short—paled in comparison to the sacrifice he'd made.

He opened his eyes, blue fire blazing from his pale face. "Liv. Thank God. I thought maybe I'd dreamed that you'd survived."

"It was no dream. You saved my life, Ford. I don't even know how to thank you," she said, tears dripping down her face despite her best efforts to stop them.

"Don't," he said, covering her hand with his, pressing it closer to his face.

"You nearly died, Ford."

"But I didn't. You didn't. We're both okay. The baby is okay. Tell me something, Livy. Did you mean what you said?"

"What did I say?"

"That you didn't want to raise our baby alone?"

"I did, but there's something that I didn't say. There's no one else I want to raise our child with but you, Ford. The past is over. I want to start fresh. The two of us together building that life I've always dreamed of."

"You're not the only one with that dream now, Olivia. When they wheeled me into surgery, you know what I was doing?"

"Telling them you were fine and trying to jump of the gurney to find me?"

"Besides that," he said, offering a smile that made Olivia's heart swell with joy. He looked like Ford again. Handsome, charming, exasperating Ford.

"What?"

"I was praying I'd get a chance to build a new life with you. One with that old Victorian you've always wanted. A white picket fence. A swing set in the backyard."

"Long walks in the evenings?"

"And church on Sunday morning. Picnics in the park. A couple of kids laughing and playing while we talk." His eyes drifted shut, and Olivia tried to slip her hand out from under his, her tears still flowing, her heart so full she thought she'd burst with the joy of it.

Ford's grip tightened and he opened his eyes.

"My body wants to rest, but my mind says that if I do, you'll disappear and I'll have to spend another four months searching the country for you."

"Rest. I'm not going anywhere," she said.

"I'm not worried about you going. I'm worried about the FBI coming and stealing you away."

"No one is going to steal anyone on my watch," Rachel cut in, her voice brusque as shoved a wad of tissues into Olivia's free hand.

"Thanks."

"No problem. Now, sit yourself down in this chair and relax while your husband sleeps. I'm going to call for a cot to be brought in, 'cause it looks to me like you could use some rest, too." She turned away before Olivia could tell her not to bother. A chair was just fine as long as she was with Ford.

She eased down into it, smiling. "Happy now?"

"More than happy. We're both alive. We're both safe."

"For now."

"Forever. I really believe that, Livy. God didn't get us through the last few days to abandon us. He'll get us through the next few weeks. Get us through the trial. And when it's over, He'll be the cornerstone of the new life we build together. How does that sound, my love?"

"It sounds perfect," Olivia responded, pressing

a kiss to Ford's lips, sealing their love, echoing his faith.

Then she leaned back, smiling into Ford's eyes until he drifted to sleep and she drifted with him, hands still connected, hearts beating in rhythm with one another. In sync as they'd never been before. Their hope for the future, their faith that God would keep them safe, filling Olivia with peace as she let the dream take her.

NINETEEN

"You two ready to head out?" Special Agent Jackson McGraw asked as Olivia and Ford were shepherded out of the courthouse. Bright May sunlight shimmered on the pavement and flashed on camera lenses aimed in her direction, but Olivia paid no attention. The trial was over. The jury would decide Vincent Martino's fate, and Olivia and Ford were finally free to begin the life they'd been planning while Ford recovered.

Olivia glanced at her husband, smiling as she responded to McGraw's question. "We've been ready for weeks."

"Yeah, I figured that," Jackson said, his gaze skimming the crowd, still searching for danger despite the trial's end. The Martino family wasn't the kind to forgive and forget. The hate-filled looks they'd shot in Olivia's direction during the trial had contrasted sharply with Vincent Martino's blank, dead-eyed stare. Just looking into his eyes had made Olivia want to cup her hands protectively over her noticeably expanding belly.

"How are you going to get us out of the city with this circus of reporters following our every move?" Ford asked, his voice gravely with worry and irritation. He'd been antsy during the trial, confident in his faith but concerned for Olivia. The trial was too stressful for a pregnant woman, he'd claimed, and Olivia had laughed.

After all they'd been through, sitting in a chair while lawyers questioned what she'd seen in December had seemed like a piece of cake.

"We're taking you back to FBI headquarters. We've got a helicopter there waiting to bring you to the airport." They also had Olivia and Ford's new identities. Jackson didn't mention it, but the truth was a warm kernel of hope in Olivia's gut. Soon she and Ford would put the horror of the past few months behind them, they'd begin a new life filled with a million possibilities.

The thought filled her with joy, and she could barely contain it as they piled into a sedan and made the ten-mile trek to the building where she and Ford had spent the last few weeks since Ford's release from the hospital. Jackson had been telling the truth when he'd said their stay would be comfortable. A large conference room in the upper level of the building had been converted into an apartment while Ford recuperated, and Ford and Olivia had been taken there as soon as Ford's doctors gave the okay for him to leave the hospital. During their short stay there, they'd almost been able to pretend they were back in early days of their marriage when an efficiency apartment and their love for each other had been more than enough.

Olivia waited impatiently while several agents approached the sedan and stood watch while Jackson opened the door. "Ready?"

"I was ready months ago," Ford muttered as he maneuvered out of the car and offered a hand to Olivia.

She accepted, excitement thrumming through her veins. A new life. A fresh start. And in just a few more months a baby.

"I can't say I'm sorry to say goodbye to this place," Ford said as they walked into the building.

"And I can't say I blame you. It's been a long and difficult road, but you two are almost at the end of it. I can't express to you how much the FBI appreciates what you've done, Olivia." Jackson responded, pressing the button on the elevator and then waiting while Olivia and Ford piled in.

"I couldn't have done anything else."

"Maybe not, but not everyone would feel the same. You're a strong woman." Jackson smiled, and Olivia sensed his relief. He'd done as he'd promised and gotten her through the trial in one piece.

"She is, isn't she?" Ford said, his arm around Olivia's shoulders. He'd healed more quickly than the doctors anticipated, surprising everyone with his swift recovery. Everyone except Olivia. She knew how determined her husband was. How focused and goal driven, and his goal had been to get better so that he and Olivia could start their new lives together.

"One of the strongest people I know," Jackson responded, something dark and troubled in his gaze. "Which reminds me—"

"Whatever it is, she's not doing it. She's testified and now we're going," Ford interrupted.

"Why don't you let me decide what I am or am not going to do?" Olivia said, and Ford smiled sheepishly.

"Sorry. I'm just a little anxious to put this place behind us."

"And you're going to, but there's someone who wanted to meet Olivia. I told her it was up to the two of you whether or not you wanted to put your trip off for a few more minutes."

"Who?" Olivia asked, curious. During the past few weeks she'd had few visitors. Jessie had come, pale and still recovering from a nearly fatal gunshot wound. Marshal James had made an appearance. Olivia's parents had been noticeably absent. Though Olivia had called to update them, neither had made the time to visit.

And that was fine with Olivia.

She had everything she'd ever wanted. She wouldn't ask for anything more.

"She's someone I've known for twenty-two years. A young lady whose life was impacted by the Martino family. She wants to meet with you to thank you for testifying against Vincent."

Olivia couldn't say no to that. She glanced at Ford and he nodded his agreement. "I'd be happy to meet with her."

"Thank you. It's going to mean a lot to Kristin. Before I take you to her, let's go over the plans for your departure. You've packed a small suitcase each?"

"Yes, and I've wired funds to an off shore account," Ford said, his arm tightening around Olivia's shoulders. She knew what he was feeling—excitement, apprehension. Joy. They were leaving the past behind completely, starting fresh in a way most people never could. Their travel plans were convoluted and besides Ford and Olivia only Marshal McGraw knew their final destination—a small city outside of Paris. Maybe they'd stay there. Maybe they'd move on. For now, though, a tiny cottage in the French countryside waited, and Olivia couldn't wait to get there.

"And you've told no one of your plans, and you realize that once you get on the helicopter you must assume your new identities. No contact with old friends or associates or family."

"We've been briefed, McGraw, so how about we just move on to the part where you wish us luck and we walk out of this place?" Ford said, and Jackson grinned.

"Sorry. Let's go. Ms. Perry is waiting right down the hall. Once you've met with her, we'll go up to the roof. The helicopter is on standby."

He pushed the door open and led them out into the corridor, past a few closed doors and to one that stood open.

"This shouldn't take long," he said as he stepped inside.

Olivia followed, Ford pressed close to her side.

A woman stood at the far side of the room, staring out one of the windows. She turned as they approached, her thick brown hair swinging with the movement.

"Olivia?" She asked, her gaze on Olivia's face, then dropping to Olivia's stomach.

"Yes," Olivia responded, offering her hand.

"I'm Kristin Perry. Jackson has told me so much about you, and I've got to admit, I've been glued to the news for the past week watching the media circus surrounding the trial."

Olivia had *been* the news for the last week, but she didn't say that, just smiled at the young woman encouragingly. "Jackson said you wanted to speak to me."

"I wanted to thank you."

"For?"

"For testifying against Vincent Martino. That took a lot of courage."

"Thank you, but as I've said to Jackson, I did what anyone would have."

"Not anyone. Only some people have it in them to go against a family like the Martinos. You're one. My mother was one," Kristin said, the sadness in her eyes unmistakable.

"Your mother?"

"She was like you. A young pregnant woman who witnessed a crime. I know she must have been scared. She wasn't fortunate enough to have someone standing beside her," Kristin said, her gaze shooting to Ford. She offered him a quick smile before continuing.

"It was just my mother, and she could have run, ignored what she'd seen and gone on with her life, but she believed in doing the right thing and she agreed to testify against the Martino family. The Martinos weren't happy about it. They attacked my mother and me, but Mom was able to save us. Unfortunately, she was so scared that I'd be killed because of her testimony, that she left me with Jackson and went into hiding. I haven't seen her since."

"I'm so sorry," Olivia said, reaching out to take Kristin's hand.

"Don't be. I wish I could have had my mother in my life for all these years, but we both survived, and I've had a good life raised by people who love me. But when I saw your story, it brought up a lot of things. I'm so glad you're going to be able to keep your baby."

"Maybe one day you'll find your mother again," Olivia said, grief for the young woman and the mother who'd left her a hard knot in her stomach. Kristin's mother must have been incredibly strong to leave her daughter behind, to sacrifice years spent with a child she loved so that that child could be safe.

"I hope so, but if I don't, at least I'll know your child has you. That the Martinos couldn't break your family apart like they did mine." She smiled, but Olivia knew she must long desperately to be reunited with her mother.

And what of her mother?

Did she grieve for the child she'd left behind? Did she celebrate each birthday with cake and tears?

Just the thought made Olivia's eyes well. Sh
blinked hard, not wanting to cry in front of Kristir
"I want you to know that Ford and I will be prayin
that you and your mother will be reunited one day.

"Thank you. That means a lot to me. And I war
you to know—" Before she could finish, Jackson'
cell phone rang. He frowned, lifting it to his ea
his scowl deepening as he listened, his muscle
visibly tensing.

"How is that possible?" His gaze rested o
Olivia, and she knew whatever he was hearin
wasn't good. "Get every available man on i
Now!" He hung up, shoving the phone away, hi
movements sharp and rigid.

"I'm afraid we're going to have to cut thi
meeting short. Something has come up."

"I don't like the look on your face, McGraw
What, exactly, has come up?" Ford asked, scowlin,
at the other man.

"We've got a problem."

"What kind of problem?"

"Vincent Martino has escaped custody."

"What? How?" Olivia and Ford asked in unison

"I don't have all the details, but it sounds like h
escaped from the hospital."

"What was he doing at the hospital? He didn'
seem sick at the trial today." As a matter of fact
Olivia had thought he'd seemed almost smug a

the jury found him guilty of murder in the first degree.

"His father is dying. His lawyer fought hard to get him a visit with the old don before Vincent went back to maximum security. Said the don was on his deathbed and that it was cruel and unusual punishment to keep the eldest child from his father's side."

"And the judge bought that?" Kristin asked, clearly disgusted.

"Every judge is a son or daughter, and most have at least a small measure of compassion," Jackson responded. "Besides, if everyone had been on the ball and doing their job, a visit to the hospital wouldn't have resulted in an escaped prisoner."

"Then how did it?" Ford pressed, and Jackson sighed, running a hand over his hair.

"A nurse was found dead in a supply closet in the basement of the hospital. There was a smudge of black on her palm."

"A smudge of black on her palm? What is that? A calling card?" Kristin asked, her brow furrowed with the same confusion Olivia felt.

"I'm afraid so," Jackson said. "We've seen it twice before on two victims that testified against the Martinos."

"You mean the women who were murdered in Montana?" Olivia asked.

"Yes. One of Martino's hired help murdered the nurse, probably soon after she arrived for her shift shoved her body in the closet and took her ID Once Vincent arrived to visit the old don, the 'nurse' pulled a gun and held a civilian hostage Fortunately, that woman wasn't hurt."

"But Martino escaped."

"Right. Kristin, if you'll wait here, I'll be back soon to escort you out. Ford. Olivia. Let's head up to the roof. It's time to start your new lives."

"But—"

"Don't argue with a good thing, Livy." Ford interrupted, gently squeezing her shoulder "Besides, there's nothing we can do to help them find Martino. You've testified. The judge will pass sentence. Leave the rest for the FBI and police."

He was right. Of course he was, and Olivia nodded as Jackson led them into stairwell and up a flight of stairs.

A helicopter waited in the center of the flat roof and a man got out as Ford and Olivia approached Dark-haired and tall, U.S. Marshal Micah McGraw looked younger and less hardened than his FBI brother. "We've got your belongings in route to the airport. Should arrive before the flight takes of Here are your new identification cards. Passport are included." He handed Olivia a brown envelope and she clutched it tight. There future lay inside

Hers. The baby's. Ford's. She wouldn't let that be marred by worries about Vincent Martino's escape.

"Thank you, Micah."

"No need to thank me. This is what I do." He flashed a smile, but his gaze was on Jackson. "I heard the news."

"I don't think there's anyone in federal law enforcement who hasn't," Jackson replied, his tone grim.

"We'll get him, bro."

"We'd better. Now, get these two to the airport and out of here. I won't rest easy until I know Olivia is far from Vincent Martino's grasp."

"Will do," Micah replied. "Come on. Let's go. You two have a new life to begin."

He gestured for Olivia and Ford to climb into the helicopter. Ford went first, then turned, to grab Olivia's hand, smiling encouragement as she clambered in after him.

"Ready?" he asked as Olivia pulled a seat belt over her burgeoning belly.

"I'm more than ready."

"Me, too, Liv. Me, too." And he leaned in to offer a kiss filled with all the promise and hope Olivia had almost stopped believing in.

She smiled, squeezing his hand, peace replacing fear. Faith replacing doubt. God had brought them this far. He wouldn't abandon them now. Soon, they'd have the new life they both craved, and the joy of that resounded through Olivia as the helicopter lifted off, speeding away from the FBI headquarters, speeding away from the past, speeding toward the only thing Olivia had ever wanted—a life filled with love.

EPILOGUE

France
Two weeks later

Olivia Jeffries scowled as she eyed her reflection in the mirror. She'd selected a pale yellow dress with an empire waist for the occasion, but it may not have been the best choice. Not only did the high waistline *not* camouflage Olivia's burgeoning belly, the loose flow of the skirt seemed to emphasize the baby's presence. She turned from side to side, flattening the material against her stomach and sighing, At least her hair looked good. She'd left it loose and curly the way Ford liked it, and the pastor's wife had helped her fashion a crown of tiny white and yellow flowers.

She looked like a flower child. A very pregnant one.

She scowled again. Maybe she should scoop her hair up into a loose bun, lose the flower crown...

A soft knock sounded at the door of the changing room and it swung open, a pretty dark-haired woman hovering in the threshold. A few years older than Olivia, Julia Pothier had met her French husband on a mission trip to Africa. They'd married a few years later and settled in his home country, planting a church an hour outside of Paris. It was a mile from the little town where Olivia and Ford had settled after they'd fled Chicago. There was no doubt Micah McGraw had known of the couple when he'd chosen where Olivia and Ford would begin their new lives. Having an American close by had made Olivia's transition easier than she'd thought it would be.

She smiled at her new friend, motioning for her to enter the room. "I think I may need to ditch these flowers."

"Why? They're beautiful, and so are you. Besides, your husband is waiting."

"Impatiently?"

"Only a little," Julia responded, smiling.

"All right. I guess I can't put it off any longer."

"Would you want to?"

"No."

"Good, because I made this just for you." Julia handed Olivia a bouquet of white and yellow roses tied with a pale yellow ribbon.

"They're beautiful. Thank you, Julia."

"Every bride needs a bouquet."

"Every bride isn't five and a half months pregnant," Olivia muttered, following Julia to heavy wood doors that opened into the nearly empty sanctuary.

Large and dimly lit, the building had been erected in the eighteenth century, abandoned in the 1970s and was now being brought back to life by the Pothiers. Over the past ten years, the couple had polished old wooden pews and wide-planked flooring. They'd replaced cracked and broken stained glass windows, and they'd filled the silent church with noise again. Their congregation was small, but growing, and Olivia knew that the future would only be brighter for the little country church.

Just as it would be for her little family.

The trial was over. Vincent Martino had been convicted, and Olivia trusted the FBI to find him and put him in prison where he belonged. The past was behind her. The future ahead. All she had to do was embrace it.

She took a deep breath, stepping into the room.

Marcus Pothier stood at the front of the church, holding a Bible and speaking quietly to Ford. He stopped talking as he caught sight of Olivia and Julia, a soft smile easing the hard lines of his face.

Ford turned, his eyes widening as he met Olivia's gaze. Her heart leaped in acknowledgment, her pulse racing with love. With joy.

He took a step toward her, might have walked the rest of the way up the aisle, but Marcus put a hand on his arm, holding him in place.

Music filled the room, soaring to the vaulted ceiling, echoing through the empty space. Not a traditional wedding march, but this wasn't a traditional wedding. It was a renewal of promises. A fresh start with the only man Olivia had ever loved.

She walked down the aisle, met her husband there. Looked into his eyes as Marcus began to speak about love, about faith, about two people coming together as one. The ceremony was simple and short, the promises she and Ford exchanged heartfelt and straightforward. To put God first and then each other. To raise their child with faith and prayer. To support each other. To be there for each other. One promise built on another, the foundation solid and sure.

When it was over, Ford pulled Olivia into his arms, kissed her deeply.

"I love you, Liv."

"I love you, too," she said, meaning it more than she'd ever imagined she could.

Faith. Love. They went hand in hand, feeding off

each other until one was the same as the other. The knowledge whispered through Olivia's mind as Ford took her hand, led her from the sanctuary, out into the warm spring day and into their future together.

* * * * *

Dear Reader,

When Olivia Jarrod sees Vincent Martino murder his rival, she's terrified but agrees to testify against him. Federal marshals assure her she's safe, but Olivia has more than herself to worry about. She's pregnant with her estranged husband, Ford Jensen's, child. Protecting their baby is her priority.

Protecting Olivia is Ford's.

He's made a lot of mistakes during their marriage, but he's determined to make things right. When he finds Olivia hiding in a small Montana town, he'll risk everything to keep her safe.

Deadly Vows is a story of peril and intrigue, but it is also a story of second chances. Like all of us, Olivia and Ford have regrets. As they face danger, they must let go of the past, forgive each other and step with faith into the future.

I hope you enjoy their story, and I pray that, like them, you will know the mercy of God's grace and the joy of the second chances He offers.

Blessings,

Shirlee McCoy

QUESTIONS FOR DISCUSSION

1. Olivia has always dreamed of having children, yet she married a man who had no desire to be a father. What drew her to Ford? Would you ever give up one of your dreams for love?

2. How strong was Olivia's faith when she met Ford?

3. Was it strengthened or weakened by their marriage?

4. As a witness under federal protection, Olivia must give up every part of her old life. That includes Ford. How does she feel about this? How would you feel if you were in her situation?

5. Does learning that she's pregnant change the way she feels about leaving her past behind her?

6. In what way does Olivia's situation make her more dependent on God?

7. Ford is attacked by Martino's henchmen, and being close to death makes him reevaluate his

priorities. What does he realize about his relationship with Olivia?

8. How does his desperation lead him closer to God?

9. Ford is shocked to learn that Olivia is pregnant. What are his reasons for not wanting to be a father? Do you think they're valid?

10. How do his feelings about fatherhood change?

11. An underlying theme of this story is forgiveness. At what point is Olivia truly able to forgive Ford for the hurt he's caused her? Have you had a hard time forgiving someone in your life? How did you overcome that?

12. The Bible tells us that we are to forgive others in the same way that God forgives us. What does this mean?

13. Why is that kind of forgiveness such a difficult thing to give?

14. What do you think will happen in the next books in the series?

*The mob is after her birth mother,
and Kristin Perry is determined
to find her first—at any cost.
Read on for a preview of
FATAL SECRETS by Barbara Phinney,
the next exciting book in the
PROTECTING THE WITNESSES series,
available in May.*

Zane Black knew Kristin Perry immediately. On Friday she'd called him, her soft, lilting voice giving him a clear impression of what she looked like, clearer than he'd ever had before with a client.

Wide green eyes blinked at him. Eyes soaked in fear.

"You *are* Kristin Perry, aren't you?" he asked.

She nodded jerkily. Finally, with one more blink, she spoke. "Yes. And you are…?"

"Zane Black, private investigator." She knew who he was, surely? She'd asked him to meet her here.

No, this wasn't quite the woman he'd spoken to on the phone, the calm, quiet woman who had sounded determined. This woman was scared, confused. It was clear she was already regretting her decision to contact him.

Zane sat down, wondering if he would get the brush-off. "You mentioned you're trying to locate a woman. Do you have her name?"

Kristin bit her lip. Zane watched the motion intently, finding it oddly attractive.

"I have very little information, I'm afraid. I know what the woman's name was years ago, and her age, but that's pretty much it."

"Is she a relative?"

Again she bit her lip. "I'd rather not say. I need you to be very discreet."

"I'm always discreet."

"No." She leaned forward, her voice dropping and her expression steeled. "I need you to find this woman without *anyone* ever knowing you're looking for her."

Can Kristin and Zane find her mother
before the mob finds them?
To find out, pick up FATAL SECRETS
by Barbara Phinney,
available in May
from Love Inspired Suspense.